Welcome to
St Piran...

Next to the rugged ... ...
lies the picturesque Cornish town of St Piran,
where you'll find a bustling hospital famed
for the dedication, talent and passion
of its staff—on and off the wards!

Under the warmth of the Cornish sun
Italian doctors, heart surgeons and
playboy princes discover that romance blossoms
in the most unlikely of places…

You'll also meet the devilishly handsome
Dr Josh O'Hara and the beautiful,
fragile Megan Phillips…and discover the secret
that tore these star-crossed lovers apart.

Turn the page to step into St Piran's—
where every drama has a dreamy doctor…
and a happy ending.

Dear Reader

Writing is a solitary occupation. Normally it's just you, your computer, or a pen and notebook for company as you set off on a new journey, a new story, so working as part of a continuity is a novelty—a decidedly nice one. It means you get the chance to 'talk' to fellow Medical™ Romance writers, to thrash out ideas, to create great linking characters, and to discover who has drunk the most coffee that day, or eaten the most sticky buns. Well, we writers need inner sustenance as well as imagination! .

Being part of the *St Piran's Hospital* series has been such a joy—not least because I grew to love both of my characters, even though there were times when I wanted to grab Connor by the lapels of his smart city suit and yell, 'Talk to Brianna, you idiot! Just tell her how you feel!'

But he can't talk to Brianna about what broke her heart, and she doesn't know how to get through to him—until they are thrown together in the Neonatal Intensive Care Unit of St Piran's Hospital in Cornwall, and then it's decision time for both of them. Have they a future together, or will they go their separate ways?

You'll have to read this book to find out, but I do hope you will enjoy reading about Connor and Brianna as much as I enjoyed writing about them.

Best wishes

Maggie Kingsley

ST PIRAN'S: TINY MIRACLE TWINS

BY
MAGGIE KINGSLEY

First published in Great Britain 2011
by Mills & Boon, an imprint of Harlequin (UK) Limited,
Eton House, 18-24 Paradise Road, Richmond, Surrey TW9 1SR

© Harlequin Books S.A. 2011

ISBN: 978 0 263 88590 3

Special thanks and acknowledgement are given to Maggie Kingsley for her contribution to the *St Piran's Hospital* series

Harlequin (UK) policy is to use papers that are natural, renewable and recyclable products and made from wood grown in sustainable forests. The logging and manufacturing process conform to the legal environmental regulations of the country of origin.

Printed and bound in Spain
by Blackprint CPI, Barcelona

Maggie Kingsley says she can't remember a time when she didn't want to be a writer, but she put her dream on hold and decided to 'be sensible' and become a teacher instead. Five years at the chalkface was enough to convince her she wasn't cut out for it, and she 'escaped' to work for a major charity. Unfortunately—or fortunately!—a back injury ended her career, and when she and her family moved to a remote cottage in the north of Scotland it was her family who nagged her into attempting to make her dream a reality. Combining a love of romantic fiction with a knowledge of medicine gleaned from the many professionals in her family, Maggie says she can't now imagine ever being able to have so much fun legally doing anything else!

Dedication

I often wonder how my sister Elizabeth puts up with my many crises of confidence when I'm writing, without ever saying to me, 'Maggie, get a grip!' or strangling me, but she does. So thank you, little sister, and this book is dedicated to you, for your patience, forbearance, and all the times you've listened to me when I've said, 'OK, do you think *this* would be better?' without running screaming from the room.

ST PIRAN'S HOSPITAL
*Where every drama has a dreamy doctor…
and a happy ending.*

*In December we gave you the first two St Piran's stories
in one month!*

**Nick Tremayne and Kate Althorp
finally got their happy-ever-after in:**
ST PIRAN'S: THE WEDDING OF THE YEAR
by Caroline Anderson

**Dr Izzy Bailey was swept off her feet
by sexy Spaniard Diego Ramirez:**
ST PIRAN'S: RESCUING PREGNANT CINDERELLA
by Carol Marinelli

**In January the arrival of sizzlingly hot
Italian neurosurgeon Giovanni Corezzi
was enough to make any woman forget the cold!**
ST PIRAN'S: ITALIAN SURGEON, FORBIDDEN BRIDE
by Margaret McDonagh

**In February daredevil doc William MacNeil
unexpectedly discovered he was a father in:**
ST PIRAN'S: DAREDEVIL, DOCTOR…DAD!
by Anne Fraser

**March saw a new heart surgeon
who had everyone's pulses racing in:**
ST PIRAN'S: THE BROODING HEART SURGEON
by Alison Roberts

**Last month fireman Tom Nicholson
stole Flora Loveday's heart in:**
ST PIRAN'S: THE FIREMAN AND NURSE LOVEDAY
by Kate Hardy

**This month, newborn twins could just bring
a marriage miracle for Brianna and Connor**
ST PIRAN'S: TINY MIRACLE TWINS
by Maggie Kingsley

**And playboy Prince Alessandro Cavalieri
honours St Piran's with a visit in June**
ST PIRAN'S: PRINCE ON THE CHILDREN'S WARD
by Sarah Morgan

CHAPTER ONE

People say time heals everything but it doesn't, not completely, never totally. Sometimes all it takes is the overheard fragment of a song, a whispered comment, or an unexpected meeting, and the scab that time has so carefully placed over the old wound begins to come apart, leaving the pain just as acute as it ever was, just as raw.

'So, the rumours are true, then,' Sister Brianna Flannigan observed as she sipped her coffee in the canteen of St Piran's. 'A troubleshooter really is coming to the hospital to see which departments should be closed?'

'And not just coming, I'm afraid.' Megan Phillips sighed. 'He's actually arriving some time today if the grapevine is correct.'

'But this is a good hospital,' Brianna protested. 'The staff are dedicated, the quality of surgery is second to none, and it provides a much-needed medical resource for the people who live in this part of Cornwall.'

'Agreed.' Jess Corezzi nodded glumly. 'But, according to the board, we're leaking money like a sieve, and…' She held up her hands and made pretend speech marks. '"Something Has to be Done".'

'But surely that doesn't have to mean ward or—heaven

forbid—complete department closures?' Brianna demanded. 'There must be some other way to save money.'

'Canning my job will probably be the first thing on this auditor's list,' Jess said ruefully. 'Counselling patients, and their families, as I do…' She shook her head. 'I can't see him regarding that as necessary.'

'But your job is vitally important,' Brianna protested, her large brown eyes troubled. 'The parents of my babies in NICU need you—'

'As do the parents, and kids in Paeds,' Megan chipped in, but Jess didn't look convinced, and Brianna could understand why.

If the auditor had been drafted in to make economies he was bound to look at the non-nursing staff first, and though she and Megan might think Jess's counselling role essential she had a horrible suspicion this money man would not.

'What does Gio think?' Brianna asked, thinking of Jess's handsome Italian husband, a neurosurgeon who had arrived at St Piran's the previous autumn and swept her friend off her feet.

'He thinks like you, that the auditor will recognise how valuable my work is and recommend shelving the new specialist paediatric burns unit instead, but frankly…' Jess shrugged. 'I can't see that happening. There is a need for that unit, plus the building is almost complete, and Admin have already asked that foreign prince to perform the grand opening in a couple of months.'

Brianna didn't think Gio's suggestion likely, either, and neither did Megan, judging by her expression.

'At least both your departments will be safe,' Jess continued bracingly. 'No one in their right mind would shut down a neonatal intensive care unit or a paediatric ward.'

Brianna could think of one man who would. One man

to whom statistics and efficiency had always been more important than people, and she shivered involuntarily.

'You OK?' Megan asked with a slight frown, and Brianna forced a smile.

'I just don't like all this talk of department closures. This hospital has been my...' She came to a halt. She had been about to say 'refuge', but though she, Jess and Megan had become friends during the two years she'd been at St Piran's there were areas of her life that were strictly off limits, and her past was one of them. 'I've been so very happy here,' she said instead.

'Me, too,' Jess replied, and Megan nodded in agreement.

'Look, do we know anything about this man?' Brianna asked. 'Where he's from, what other hospitals he's been to?'

'All we know is he's from London,' Jess replied, and the shiver Brianna had felt earlier became more pronounced.

'London?' she echoed. 'Jess—'

The insistent bleep of a pager brought her to a halt. All three women instantly reached for theirs, but it was Megan who got to her feet with a groan.

'Nothing wrong in Paeds, I hope?' Brianna said, and Megan shook her head.

'It's Admin. They've got themselves in a real flap about this visitation. Yesterday they wanted everything in duplicate. Now they've decided they want everything in triplicate.'

With a rueful smile the paediatric specialist registrar headed off towards the canteen exit but, as Brianna and Jess watched her, the door suddenly opened and Josh O'Hara, the consultant from A and E, appeared. He clearly said something to Megan, actually put out his hand to stay her, but she pushed past him without a word, and Brianna and Jess exchanged glances.

'The atmosphere's not getting any better between those two, is it?' Brianna said, and Jess sighed.

'I guess it can't. Not when Josh is married to Rebecca, and Megan's most certainly not a home-wrecker.'

'Has…?' Brianna cleared her throat awkwardly. 'Has she said anything to you about him?'

'I only know there's a past history there, not what it is, and I wouldn't dream of asking,' Jess replied. 'My guess is they were an item years ago, before Josh got married, but as to what happened or why they split up…' The hospital counsellor lifted her shoulders helplessly. 'I just wish he hadn't taken the consultant's job in A and E. OK, so he didn't know Megan would be working at St Piran's, but can you imagine how awful it must be, having someone you once loved reappear in your life like this?'

Brianna could. She didn't want to imagine it, but she could, all too vividly.

Secrets, she thought as she watched Josh walk slowly across the canteen then stare unenthusiastically at the lunch menu. She, Jess and Megan, all of them had secrets. Maybe that's what had drawn them together, made them friends. That, and the fact they never pried into one another's private lives so she'd had no idea until a few months ago that Jess had HIV, or that Megan was nursing a badly broken heart, while neither of them knew she…

Don't go there, Brianna, she told herself. *Don't go there, not ever.*

'The annoying thing is, I like him,' Jess continued as Josh picked up a doughnut and coffee, then morosely went to sit at an empty table near the back of the canteen. 'Whatever happened between him and Megan in the past, I still think he's one of the good guys.'

'And does your husband know you consider Josh "one of the good guys"?' Brianna asked, her brown eyes dancing, and the counsellor laughed.

'Gio knows I only have eyes for him,' she replied. 'I just wish…this situation between Megan and Josh… I just wish there was something I could do to help.'

Brianna wished she could, too, as she and Jess left the canteen and went their separate ways. She'd liked Josh O'Hara from the very first minute she'd met him. For sure he'd teased her when he'd discovered she was from Ireland as he was, had said that with her long, auburn hair she reminded him of the 1940s Hollywood actress, Maureen O'Hara, but she knew he hadn't been hitting on her. He was just a natural-born charmer, adept at making people feel at ease. Unless, of course, that person was Megan Phillips, she thought with a deep sigh.

And she could have done with Josh at her side, dispensing a whole bucketload of his charm, she decided as she swiped her ID card to gain entry to NICU, only to walk straight into Rita, NICU's ward clerk, and her least favourite member of staff in the hospital.

'I'm not late back from lunch, Rita,' Brianna said, consulting her watch pointedly, 'the unit doesn't appear to be on fire, I'm sure you would have paged me if any of the babies was giving cause for concern, so can I assume you want to report one of the nursing staff for some petty infringement?'

'He's here,' the NICU ward clerk hissed. 'The auditor. He arrived half an hour ago, and I've got him in my office, looking at some files, but I don't know how long I can keep him there.'

'Have you considered chains, manacles, possibly a straitjacket?'

'This is not a laughing matter, Sister Flannigan,' Rita retorted. 'Mr Brooke is still in Theatre—'

'Which is probably just as well,' Brianna interrupted. 'Letting Babbling loose amongst walking, healthy people...' She shook her head. 'Not a good idea.'

'Neither is referring to our head of department by that stupid nickname,' Rita protested, apparently conveniently forgetting that she called their consultant Mr Brooke 'Babbling' just as often as the rest of the staff in NICU did.

'Rita—'

'First impressions count, Sister, and we've already got off to a bad one with Mr Brooke not being here to meet the VIP.'

'Yes, it really was *very* inconsiderate of little Amy Renwick to get so sick, wasn't it?' Brianna said dryly, but her sarcasm was lost on the ward clerk.

'It certainly couldn't have happened at a worse time,' Rita agreed. 'I only have two years left to work before I retire and the last thing I want is the unit closing down before I'm ready to go.'

Yeah, and you're all heart, Rita, Brianna thought, but she didn't say that.

'I very much doubt anyone would ever contemplate shutting down a neonatal intensive care unit,' she said, deliberately echoing Jess's optimistic words, but Rita wasn't placated.

'We're grossly understaffed,' the ward clerk declared, her tightly permed grey curls practically bristling with indignation, 'and this auditor is bound to notice. Lord knows, I'm not one to complain—'

You never do anything but, Brianna thought irritably. In fact, it would be a red-letter, stop-press, post-it-to-the-world-on-Twitter day if Rita managed to get through one day without complaining.

'And no-one can say I'm not doing my best,' Rita continued, 'but, without a nurse unit manager, I'm fighting an uphill battle.'

Brianna was sorely tempted to tell the woman she might find her job considerably easier if she didn't spend half her time prying into everyone else's business and the other half spreading gossip, but the trouble was the ward clerk was right. They *were* finding it tough without a nurse unit manager, and though Admin had promised to advertise the post after Diego Ramirez returned to Spain, there had been no sign yet of them doing anything.

'I'm sure the auditor will make allowances for us,' she declared, 'and now, if you'll excuse me—'

'Selfish, that's what I call it,' Rita continued. 'Mr Ramirez leaving us all in the lurch. In my day people had a sense of duty, a sense of responsibility, but nobody cares about standards nowadays. Look at all the unmarried mothers we get in NICU. Feckless, the lot of them. In my day—'

'I'm sure every family behaved like the Waltons, and nothing bad ever happened,' Brianna interrupted tersely, 'but right now, if you're so anxious about making a good impression, wouldn't it be better if you simply got on with your job?'

Rita's mouth fell open, she looked as though she'd dearly like to say something extremely cutting, then she strode away with a very audible sniff, and Brianna gritted her teeth.

She would undoubtedly pay later for what she'd said— Rita would make sure of that—but the ward clerk had caught her on the raw today. Actually, if she was honest,

Rita always caught her on the raw with her 'holier than thou' attitude to life.

'Walk a mile in my moccasins.'

It was one of her mother's favourite sayings, and her mother was right, Brianna thought as she washed her hands thoroughly then applied some antiseptic gel to ensure she didn't carry any bacteria into the unit, except…

She bit her lip as she caught sight of her reflection in the small mirror over the sink. 'The country mouse'. That was what her colleagues had called her when she'd been a student nurse, but that had been fourteen years ago. She wasn't a country mouse any more. She was thirty-two years old, the senior sister in a neonatal intensive care unit, and time and life had changed her. Especially the last two years.

Don't, Brianna, she told herself as she felt her heart twist inside her. *Don't start looking back, you can't, you mustn't, not now, not ever.*

And normally she didn't, she thought as she took a steadying breath before tucking a stray strand of her auburn hair back into its neat plait, only to realise her hand was shaking. Normally she lived in the now, determinedly refusing to look back, or forward, and it was all the fault of this damned auditor. His arrival was upsetting everyone, turning what had been her refuge into a place of uncertainty, and she didn't want uncertainty. She wanted the hospital to stay exactly as it was. Her haven, her sanctuary, her escape from all that had happened.

'Blasted number-cruncher,' she muttered as she used her elbow to push open the door leading into the NICU ward. 'Why can't he just go away and play on a motorway?'

'You wouldn't be talking about our esteemed visitor, would you?' Chris, her senior staff nurse, chuckled, clearly overhearing her.

'Got it in one,' Brianna replied, feeling herself beginning

to relax as the familiar heat in the unit enveloped her, and she heard the comforting, steady sound of beeping monitors and ventilators. 'Anything happen over lunch I should know about?'

'Mr Brooke's not back from Theatre yet and neither is Amy Renwick.'

'So Rita told me,' Brianna replied. 'It looks as though he's had to remove part of Amy's intestine after all.'

It was what they'd all been hoping the consultant wouldn't have to do. Amy Renwick had been born twelve weeks premature, and scarcely a month later she'd been diagnosed with necrotising enterocolitis. The condition wasn't uncommon in premature babies—their intestines were frequently insufficiently developed to handle digestion—but generally it could be controlled with antibiotics. In Amy's case, however, the antibiotics hadn't worked. Mr Brooke had thought he might only have to drain the infected fluid from her stomach, but, from the length of time he'd been in Theatre, it looked very much as though that solution hadn't proved to be an option.

'Is Mrs Renwick here?' Brianna asked, and the staff nurse nodded.

'She's in the parents' restroom—very upset, of course—but her family's with her.'

And they'd been a tower of strength over the past few weeks for Naomi and her husband, Brianna thought as she lifted a file from the nurses' station. Not all of their parents were so lucky. Some families lived too far away to provide emotional support, while other families simply couldn't deal with the constant up-and-down pressures of having a very premature baby.

And sometimes the people, the person, you were so sure you could depend on let you down, she thought with a sudden, unwanted, shaft of pain.

'You OK, Brianna?'

The staff nurse was gazing uncertainly at her, and Brianna manufactured a smile.

'You're the second person to ask me that today, and I'm fine,' she replied. 'I've just got a bad attack of Monday blues, not helped by the imminent arrival of this blasted auditor—'

'Who, if I'm not very much mistaken, has just arrived with Babbling and Rita,' the staff nurse warned in an undertone. 'And, if that *is* him, he looks scary. Good looking in a designer-suited, high-powered sort of way, but most definitely scary.'

Quickly, Brianna glanced over her shoulder, and in that split second her world stood still. Dimly, she heard their NICU consultant introduce the man at his side as Connor Monahan, but she didn't need the introduction. The six-foot-one rangy frame, the thick black hair and startling blue eyes, the expensive city suit and equally top-of-the-range laptop that he was carrying... It was the man she hadn't thought about—had refused to allow herself think about—for the past two years, and the file she'd been holding slipped from her nerveless fingers and landed on the floor with a clatter.

From beside her she heard Chris's small gasp of surprise at her unusual clumsiness, saw Mr Brooke's glare of irritation, but what pierced her to the core as she quickly retrieved the file then straightened up was the way the familiar blue eyes had flashed instantly from recognition to anger. How those same blue eyes were now boring deep into her, tearing her heart apart just as it had been torn apart two years ago.

'I can assure you my staff are not normally so clumsy, Mr Monahan,' she heard Mr Brooke declare, and saw Connor shake his head dismissively.

'Accidents happen,' he replied, 'and, please, everyone, call me Connor. I'm not here to judge anyone. My visit to this hospital is merely as an observer, to find out how a hospital like this serves its local community.'

'Yeah, right,' Chris muttered. 'And like we don't all know that he's been sent in to find out which department should be closed, so he can give up on the "let's all be friends" routine. And, oh, Lord, Mr Brooke is now insisting on introducing everyone,' the staff nurse continued, rolling her eyes heavenwards. 'What's the bet he won't remember half our names?'

Brianna didn't care if the middle-aged consultant did or not. She was too busy keeping her eyes fixed firmly on the file in her hand, wishing she was anywhere but here, but, out of the corner of her eye, she could see the inexorable approach of a pair of mirror-bright black shoes, could smell an all-too-distinctive sandalwood aftershave, and she sucked in an uneven breath, willing this moment to be over.

'And this is Sister Flannigan,' Mr Brooke announced when he drew level with her.

'Sister Flannigan,' Connor repeated slowly, and Brianna winced as she reluctantly raised her head to look up at him.

Never would she have imagined anyone could put quite so much sarcasm into her surname, but Connor just had.

'She's only been with us for two years,' Mr Brooke continued, clearly completely oblivious to the atmosphere, 'but since then she's become an indispensable member of the team.'

At any other time Brianna would have savoured the praise from the portly consultant, who never gave anyone any, but not today, not when she saw Connor's left eyebrow rise.

'So, you've been living here in Cornwall for the last two years, have you, Sister Flannigan?' he said with deliberate emphasis, and Brianna clasped the file in her hands even tighter.

Don't, she wanted to say. *Please, don't. Not here, not in front of everyone.* But she couldn't say anything, not with her boss listening, not with Rita's eyes darting avidly between her and Connor, her mind clearly already whirring away with speculation.

'Yes, I've been here for two years,' she muttered, 'and now if you'll excuse me…'

'Oh, absolutely not,' Connor declared, his voice ice-cold and implacable. 'In fact, I *insist* you stay.'

Had he always been quite so tall, so intimidating? she wondered as she involuntarily took a step back. Of course he had. He couldn't possibly have grown since she'd last seen him, and he'd always possessed an air of authority and power, and yet she felt transported back in time to the little country mouse she'd once been, and she hated feeling that way.

'I'm afraid you really will have to excuse me,' she said, putting as much defiance into her voice as she could muster. 'I have babies to attend to, and I also need to talk to the mother of one of our patients. Her daughter has just undergone major surgery—'

'From which we are hopeful she will make a full recovery,' Mr Brooke interrupted. 'Of course, the next few days will be critical, as I will explain to Mrs Renwick myself.'

Which is exactly what I *don't* want you to do, Brianna thought unhappily. Of course, all operations carried risks, but not for nothing had the nursing staff in NICU nicknamed their consultant 'Babbling' Brooke. Brilliant surgeon though he might be, he would persist in constantly—and at great length—giving parents the worst-case scenario possible, terrifying them witless in the process. Megan would have handled Naomi Renwick so much better, but Megan wasn't here.

'It would be no trouble for me to talk to Mrs Renwick, Mr Brooke,' she said desperately. 'I could go now—'

'Not running away from me, are you, Sister Flannigan?' Connor said, and she bit her lip savagely.

Had she been the only one in the unit who had heard the unspoken word *again* in his comment? She hoped she was, she prayed she was.

'Of course not,' she replied. 'I just… I know Mrs Renwick very well… I'm her daughter's primary carer—'

'And I'm her daughter's surgeon, and head of this department, so I will speak to her,' Mr Brooke interrupted with a finality that told Brianna there was no point in arguing. 'Now, Connor, I'm sure our ward clerk will be only too happy to let you examine more of our files—'

'Which I'm sure would be absolutely fascinating,' Connor interrupted, 'but I'm only going to be in St Piran's for the next six weeks so what I'd like to do in NICU, over the next few days, is interview all of your staff individually. Form an idea from them of how they think they fit into this unit, what their duties are, gain the bigger picture, if you like.'

Six weeks? Brianna thought, glancing from Connor to Mr Brooke with ill-disguised horror. Connor was going to be in the hospital for *six weeks*? Even if he only spent a few days in NICU, it was going to be a few days too many and Mr Brooke clearly thought the same.

'I really don't see why there's any need for you to interview my staff when I can give you the bigger picture immediately,' he said. 'Sick babies come in here, my nursing staff and I attempt to make them better. End of story.'

Brianna could have kissed the consultant, but Connor

merely smiled the smile of a man who had no intention of having his intentions thwarted.

'I still want to speak to your staff,' he insisted evenly. 'My interviews will take no longer than half an hour, and after that I will simply be a silent observer. In fact, I doubt you'll even notice I'm here.'

I'll notice, Brianna thought, desperately praying their consultant would feel the same but, to her dismay, he had clearly become bored with the conversation and simply shrugged.

'Fine—whatever,' he said. 'Just don't get in my way, or the way of my staff. So, who do you want to interview first?'

Connor made a show of glancing over the assembled nurses, but Brianna knew who he was going to choose, just as she knew Connor knew it, too.

'I'm sure Sister Flannigan and I will find a lot to talk about,' he declared with a smile that didn't even remotely suggest it would ever reach his eyes. 'Mr Brooke, do you have an office or room I could use as a base while I'm here at the hospital?'

He wanted to use NICU as his base? Even when he was assessing other departments he would keep returning to NICU as his base? *No*, Brianna thought desperately, dear heavens, *no*.

'I'll get Maintenance to clear out the nurse unit manager's office for you,' the consultant replied vaguely. 'It's not in use at the moment, but there are confidential files in it that will have to be secured, so in the meantime you could use the nurses' staffroom if you want.'

Connor nodded.

'Sounds good to me,' he said.

It didn't sound good to Brianna, and neither did the way Connor shadowed her all the way out of the ward and down the corridor as though he was convinced she might bolt. And she would have bolted, she thought, if she hadn't known that a pair of five-foot-two-inch legs could never have outrun the six-foot-one-inch legs of the man at her side.

'Would you like some tea, coffee?' she said, walking quickly over to the kettle as soon as they entered the staff-room, desperate to delay the inevitable for as long as possible. 'There's some herbal tea here, too, though I can't vouch for it being drinkable, and hot chocolate—'

'So, is it still *Brianna* Flannigan,' he interrupted, 'or did you change your Christian name as well as your surname?'

She stared at the cork board which one of the nurses had affixed to the wall above the kettle and cups. Postcards from far-away places were pinned to it, along with old birthday cards and congratulation cards, and there was also a whole array of cartoons that should have been funny but she had never felt less like laughing.

'I…I kept my Christian name,' she muttered, mechanically switching on the kettle and spooning some coffee into a cup, though she didn't really want anything. 'Flannigan was my mother's maiden name.'

'But not yours,' he said. 'You do realise I could get you fired for working at this hospital under a false name?'

He could, she knew he could, but suddenly she didn't care. Suddenly she felt cornered, and defeated, and wearily she turned to face him.

'OK, get me fired,' she said. 'If that's what you want to do, then go ahead and do it.'

'Of course that's not what I want!' he exclaimed, tossing his laptop onto the nearest seat. 'What do you take me for?'

I don't know, she thought as she gazed up into his cold,

rigid face. *I don't know because I feel like I don't know you any more, and I'm wondering now if I ever did.*

'Look, can we sit down?' she said. 'You standing there—looming over me like some spectre of doom—isn't helping.'

With a muttered oath he sat down, and, after a moment's hesitation she abandoned the kettle and took the seat opposite him.

'You really were determined I wouldn't find you, weren't you?' he said, his blue eyes fixed on her, daring her to contradict him. 'Changing your surname, moving to a one-horse town in the back of beyond in Cornwall.'

'Connor, it wasn't like that—'

'Wasn't it?' he interrupted, his voice dripping sarcasm. 'So how—exactly—would you interpret it?'

'I wanted…' Oh, but this was so hard to explain, and she wanted to explain, for him to understand. 'I just wanted…' Her voice broke slightly despite her best efforts to keep it level. 'Some peace. All I wanted was some peace.'

'And to get that you had to walk out on me?' he said incredulously. 'Walk out without a word?'

'I left you a letter,' she protested, and saw his lip curl with derision.

'"I need to be on my own for a while,"' he quoted. '"I need some space, some time to get myself together". That's hardly an "I'm leaving you, and I'm never coming back", dear-John letter, is it?'

'Connor—'

'You applied for this job without telling me, didn't you?' he said. 'You applied for it, and got it, and yet you never said a word to me about what you were planning to do.'

She swallowed hard. 'Yes.'

'So that's why you only ever took three hundred pounds out of our joint bank account,' he declared, fury deepening his voice. 'You didn't need any more money because you had this job to come to.'

'Yes,' she whispered.

'Why, Brianna, *why*?' he demanded, thrusting his fingers through his black hair, anger, hurt and bewilderment plain on his face. 'I thought we were happy, I thought you loved me.'

'Things…things haven't been right between us for a long time, Connor,' she replied, 'you know they haven't—'

'That's nonsense,' he retorted, and she clasped her hands together tightly, desperately trying to find the words that would make him understand.

'I was going under, Connor,' she cried. 'After what happened—you wouldn't talk to me, you wouldn't let me talk, and I knew—if I didn't get away—I was going to slide further and further into the black pit I'd fallen into, and if I kept on falling…' She took an uneven breath. 'I was scared—so scared—that I would never be able to get myself out again.'

'And me—what about me?' he exclaimed, his blue eyes blazing. '*Two years*, Brianna, it's been *two years* since you left and in all that time you never once lifted the phone to tell me you were OK, never once even sent me a scribbled postcard to say you were alive.'

'I was going to write, to tell you where I was,' she declared defensively, but had she really been going to? It wasn't something she wanted to think about, far less face. It was enough of a shock to see him sitting there in front of her. 'Connor—'

'You left your phone behind, the house keys, the police wouldn't help me—'

'You went to the police?' She gasped, her eyes large with dismay, and he threw her a look that made her shrink back into her seat.

'What the hell did you expect me to do? Did you think I'd simply stay home in our flat, night after night, watching TV, thinking, Well, I expect Brianna will come back eventually? *Of course* I went to the police. I thought…' He closed his eyes for a second, and when he spoke again his voice was rough. 'I thought you might have done something…stupid, but they said as you'd left a note, and your parents knew you were safe, it wasn't a police matter but a domestic one.'

'I'm sorry,' she murmured. 'I didn't realise—I never imagined you'd go to the police—'

'Can you imagine how that made me feel?' he said, his lips curving into a bitter travesty of a smile. 'When the police told me your parents knew where you were, but I didn't? I went back to Ireland, to your parents' farm in Killarney, thinking you might have gone there, and, when I discovered you hadn't, I begged them to give me your address, even your phone number, so I could at least hear your voice, know you truly were safe, but they wouldn't give me either. They said you'd made them promise not to tell me anything, that you would contact me when you were ready.'

'I'm sorry, so sorry,' she repeated, willing him to believe her. 'I didn't…' She shook her head blindly. 'I wasn't thinking clearly, not then. I just…'

'Had to get away from me,' he finished for her bitterly, and she bit her lip hard.

'Connor, listen to me—'

'Every time I heard on the news that a body had been found in some secluded spot I feared it was you,' he continued as though she hadn't spoken. 'Every time someone was pulled out of the Thames I thought, Please, don't let it be Brianna, but, as time went on, God help me, I sometimes…' He took a breath. 'Sometimes I hoped it *was* you because at least then the waiting would be over. All I needed…all I wanted…was to know you really were safe, and yet you denied me even that, Brianna.'

'I would have called you, I would have talked to you,' she said, her voice trembling, 'but I knew talking to you wouldn't help, that you wouldn't listen.'

'How can you say that?' he demanded angrily. 'Of course I would have talked, of course I would have listened!'

'You didn't before when I needed you to,' she said before she could stop herself. 'All you ever did was cut me off, change the subject, or you'd ask me…' She swallowed convulsively, hearing the tears in her voice, and she didn't want to cry…she so didn't want to cry. 'You kept asking me what was wrong, and I thought I'd go mad if you asked me that one more time because it was so obvious to me that everything was always going to be wrong, that it was never going to be right.'

'You're not making any sense—'

'Because you're not *listening*, just like you always don't,' she flared. 'Whenever I try to talk to you, you never ever *listen.*'

'Well, I want to talk now,' he countered. 'To talk properly with no lies, deception or half-truths, only honesty.'

She knew he was right, but talking honestly meant resurrecting everything that had happened, meant having to face it again. She hadn't forgotten, she never would, but over the past two years she'd managed to come to a kind of acceptance, and to talk about it now… She didn't think her heart could take that, and she shook her head.

'Connor, this isn't the time, or the place.'

'Then *when*, Brianna?' he exclaimed, and there was such a lacerating fury in his blue eyes that she winced. 'When will be the time, or the place?'

She wanted to say, *Never—nowhere.* She wanted even

more to say she wished he had never come, had never found her, but she didn't have the courage.

'I don't know,' she said wretchedly. 'I don't—'

She bit off the rest of what she had been about to say. The door of the nurses' staffroom had opened, and Megan's head had appeared hesitantly round it.

'I'm really sorry,' the paediatric specialist registrar began, glancing from Brianna to Connor, then back again, 'but I'm afraid Brianna is needed in the unit.'

Brianna was hurrying towards Megan before she had even finished speaking, but when she reached the door she heard Connor clear his throat.

'We have to talk, Brianna, and talk soon,' he said.

She thought she nodded, but she couldn't be sure. All she knew was she had to get away from him, and she was halfway down the corridor before Megan caught up with her.

'Brianna—'

'Is it Amy Renwick? Is she back from Recovery, and there's a problem, or—?'

'Actually, I'm afraid I lied, and you're not needed in the unit at all,' Megan interrupted, looking shamefaced. 'It's just…I was passing the nurses' staffroom and I heard the auditor yelling at you. I wasn't eavesdropping, honestly I wasn't,' she continued as Brianna stared at her in alarm. 'It's just the walls in this place are so thin, and you sounded… Well, you sounded really upset, and in need of rescue.'

'I did—I was,' Brianna said with a small smile.

'I think you should make a formal complaint,' Megan declared angrily. 'It's one thing to inspect a unit, to ask the staff questions about how it's run, but harassing someone…' She shook her head. 'That's completely out of order.'

'Megan, I don't want to make a complaint,' Brianna

replied. 'My interview is over, done with, so let's just leave it, OK?'

'Not on your life,' the paediatric registrar insisted. 'If this Connor whatever his name is—'

'Monahan. His name's Connor Monahan.'

'Thinks he can ride roughshod over the nursing staff, upset them, then he can think again. I can understand why you might be reluctant to make a complaint, but I'm not. I'm more than willing to march up to Admin right now, and tell them they'd better warn him to back off or they'll have the nurses' union on their doorstep.'

Megan would do it, too, Brianna thought, seeing the fury in her friend's face, and it was the last thing she wanted. It was hard enough for her to deal with Connor's reappearance in her life without having the staff in Admin gossiping about it after they'd been told all the facts, and she would have to tell them all the facts.

'Megan, it's got nothing to do with the nursing staff, or the unit,' she said unhappily. 'It's me. It's to do with me. You see, Connor Monahan and I... We know one another.'

Her friend gazed at her blankly for a second, then a look of horrified realisation appeared on her face.

'Oh, lord, he's not an ex-boyfriend of yours, is he?' she exclaimed. 'Oh, Brianna, I'm so sorry, what a nightmare for you.'

'A nightmare, for sure.' Brianna nodded. 'But you see...' She took a deep breath. 'The trouble is, Connor isn't an ex-boyfriend. He...he's my husband.'

CHAPTER TWO

'BUT Mr Brooke said yesterday—after Amy's operation—that she might need another operation,' Naomi Renwick said, her eyes dark with fear. 'He said he wouldn't know for the next seventy-two hours whether he'd successfully removed all of the infection, so you'd be keeping a very careful eye on her.'

'Which I would be doing whether Amy had been operated on or not,' Brianna replied, wishing the ever-pessimistic consultant to the darkest reaches of hell. 'Naomi, your daughter is doing very well. We have no reason to think she will require another operation—'

'But if she does… She's so little, Sister, so very little, and if she needs another operation…'

'We'll deal with it just as we've dealt with all the other problems Amy has faced since she was born a month ago. Naomi, listen to me,' Brianna continued, as Amy's mother made to interrupt. 'I can't give you any guarantees—no one can, but, please, *please*, don't go looking for bridges to cross. Amy's temperature's normal, her colour's good. In fact,' she added, 'just look at her.'

Naomi Renwick gazed down into the incubator where her daughter was vigorously kicking her little legs despite the fine line of sutures across her stomach, and her lips curved into a shaky smile.

'She's beautiful, isn't she?' she said, and Brianna nodded.

'She is, and right now she's in the best possible place, getting the best possible care, so hold onto that, OK?'

Brianna hoped Naomi Renwick would, but she wished even more, as she turned to discover Connor standing behind her, that her husband would dog some other nurse's footsteps, if only for a little while.

Twenty-four hours, she thought as she began walking down the ward, all too conscious he was following her. Just twenty-four hours ago her life might not exactly have been perfect, but at least she hadn't felt permanently besieged. Now she felt cornered, under attack, and it wasn't just by his presence, or his continual questions about the unit. It was the way he managed to somehow incorporate so many barbed comments into what he was saying that was wearing her down, little by little, bit by bit.

'How many incubators does the NICU at Plymouth have?' he asked, and she came to a weary halt.

'Twelve,' she replied, 'which is double our capacity, but their hospital covers a far greater area and population than St Piran's, so it's bound to be bigger.'

'I also notice from your ward clerk's files that every baby has a primary carer,' he continued. 'That doesn't seem to be a very efficient system in terms of time or personnel.'

'Not everything can be measured in terms of time management, or personnel distribution,' she said acidly. 'Especially the care of very vulnerable babies.'

'I see,' he said, but she doubted whether he did as she watched him type something into his state-of-the-art phone, which could probably have made him a cup of coffee if he'd asked it to.

Figures, statistics had always been his passion, not people, and he didn't seem to have changed.

'Connor—'

'Does this unit normally have quite so many unused incubators?' he asked, gesturing towards the two empty ones at the end of the ward.

'There's no such thing as "normal" in NICU,' she protested. 'We've had occasions when only three of our incubators have been in use, times when we were at full capacity, and last Christmas we were so busy we had to send babies to Plymouth because we just couldn't accommodate them. It was tough for everyone, especially the families.'

'It would be.' He nodded. 'Christmas being the time when most families like to be together.'

And you've missed two with me. He didn't say those words—he didn't need to—but she heard them loud and clear.

'Things don't always work out the way we planned,' she muttered, 'and babies can't be expected to arrive exactly when you want them to.'

'Not babies, no. Grown-ups, on the other hand,' he added, his eyes catching and holding hers, 'have a choice.'

And you chose to walk away from me. That was what he was really saying, and she swallowed painfully.

'Connor, please,' she said with difficulty. 'This is a good unit, an efficient unit. Please don't make this personal.'

His eyebrows rose. 'You think that's what I'm doing?'

'I *know* it is,' she cried. 'Look, I can understand you being angry—'

'I'm sorry to interrupt,' Rita interrupted, looking anything but as she joined them, 'but I'm afraid we've had a complaint about your car, Sister Flannigan.'

'A complaint?' Brianna echoed in confusion, and Rita smiled.

A smile that was every bit as false as the sympathetic sigh with which she followed it.

'You've parked it in the consultants' side of the car park today instead of the nurses'. Easily done, of course, when you're stressed—'

'I'm not stressed—'

'Of course you are, my dear,' Rita declared, her face all solicitous concern, but her eyes, Brianna noticed, were speculative, calculating. 'How can you possibly not be when you're doing two jobs?'

'Sister Flannigan has two jobs?' Connor frowned, and Rita nodded.

'Our nurse unit manager returned to Spain a few months back, and, as Admin haven't yet appointed his replacement, Sister Flannigan has had to temporarily step into the breach, which is probably why we're not as efficient as we should be.'

'I can't say I've noticed any inefficiency on Sister Flannigan's part,' Connor replied, attempting to walk on, but Rita was not about to be rebuffed.

'Oh, please don't think I'm suggesting Sister Flannigan is inefficient—'

Yeah, right, Rita, Brianna thought angrily, and this is clearly payback time because I chewed your head off yesterday.

'But when you're as much of a perfectionist as I am,' the ward clerk continued, all honeyed sweetness, 'I do like everything to be just so.'

'Which makes me wonder why you're still standing here,' Connor declared, 'and not back in your office, dotting some i's and crossing some t's.'

The ward clerk's mouth opened and closed soundlessly for a second, then she clamped her lips together tightly.

'Well, no one can ever accuse me of remaining where

I'm not wanted,' she said, before stomping away, and Brianna sighed.

'Which, unfortunately, isn't true.' She glanced up at Connor hesitantly. 'Thanks for saying what you did, for backing me up.'

For a moment he said nothing, then his lips twisted into something like a smile. 'I thought I always did. I thought we were a team.'

They had been once, she remembered. There had been a time when she couldn't have imagined her life without him, and then, little by little, things had changed, and two years ago...

'I'm sorry, Connor,' she murmured, 'so sorry.'

'Sorry you left, or sorry I found you?'

His eyes were fixed on her, and the awful truth was she couldn't give him an answer, not without hurting him, and she backed away from him, afraid he would realise it.

'The car,' she said haltingly. 'I have to...I need to move my car.'

She was gone before he could stop her and, when the ward door clattered shut behind her, Connor clenched his fists until his knuckles showed white.

She hadn't answered him. He'd asked her a simple, easy-to-answer question, and yet she hadn't answered him, and he needed—wanted—answers.

Dammit, she owed him that at least, he thought furiously. When he'd first seen her yesterday, his initial reaction had been to thank God she was safe, his Brianna was safe, but then anger had consumed him. A blazing, blinding, irrational anger that she could be standing in front of him looking better than he'd seen her look in a long time, had been living happily in Cornwall for the last two years, when he'd been to hell and back, fearing the worst. And she'd disappear out of his life again in an instant given half a chance. He'd seen it in her dark brown eyes, in the way she looked at him.

Well, she wasn't going to walk away from him a second time, he decided. This time he wanted answers, proper answers, and not some nonsense about him never talking to her, never listening, and he headed for the ward door to follow her.

'I'm really very sorry about this, Sister Flannigan,' Sid, the hospital handyman, said uncomfortably after she'd moved her car out of the consultants' bay and into the nurses' part of the car park. 'To be honest, I don't think there should be any divisions in the car park, but some consultants…' He shook his head. 'It's a status thing for them, you see.'

'It's all right, Sid, truly it is,' Brianna said quickly. 'I don't know where my brain was this morning…' Well, she did know—it was on Connor, she'd been thinking about Connor, and how she didn't want to meet him again, but she wasn't about to share that even with someone as nice as their handyman. 'So could you please tell whoever it was who complained that it won't happen again?'

The middle-aged handyman didn't look any happier. In fact, she could hear him muttering under his breath, 'Officious twit…that's what he is,' as he walked away, and she smiled, but, as she closed her car door, her smile vanished.

It would be so easy to simply get back into her car, and drive away. No one would miss her for a while, and if she kept on driving, and driving, she might eventually reach a place where Connor would never find her. She could start again, change her name again, and—

'Don't, Brianna,' a feminine voice said gently. 'I know what you're thinking, and it won't solve anything.'

'It might,' Brianna muttered, as she turned to see Jess watching her.

'Megan told me about Connor being your husband. She wouldn't normally break a confidence—you know she wouldn't,' the counsellor added quickly as Brianna stared at her in alarm, 'but she's worried about you.'

'I know, but…' Brianna shook her head. 'Jess, have you ever wanted to run away? To just run away, leave everything behind, and start all over?'

'I did—I have,' the counsellor replied. 'When the staff at the hospital I worked in before I came to St Piran's found out about me having HIV…a lot of them cut me dead, crossed the street to avoid me—'

'Oh, Jess!'

'And I couldn't bear it so I ran, and then…' She sighed, a low, sad sigh. 'Well, you know what happened. That reporter from the *Penhally Gazette* broadcast my condition all over his newspaper, and I wanted to run again, but I knew if I did, I would be leaving behind the people, the hospital I felt I'd become such a part of.'

'And Gio,' Brianna murmured. 'You would have been leaving him behind, too.'

'I had no guarantees he would stand by me when he found out the truth, Brianna. He could have walked away and, if he had, then I…' Jess managed a watery smile. 'I would just have to have lived with it.'

Brianna stared down at the car keys in her hand.

'I don't know if I'm as strong as you are.'

'I think you are,' Jess said softly, 'but it's your choice, Brianna. You can stay and confront your fear, or you can run, but if you do run don't forget that whatever you're scared of won't go away. It will always be there, like a dark shadow hanging over you.'

Her friend was right, she knew she was. Running wasn't

the answer, but to stay and try to get Connor to talk to her, to really talk…

'Jess…' she began, only to look sharply round with a frown. 'Did you hear that?'

'Hear what?' Jess said in confusion. 'I can hear the traffic, the birds in the trees—'

'It's a baby. A baby in distress, and it's close by.'

Jess stared at her as though she was suddenly having grave doubts about her mental stability but, having worked with babies for most of her adult life, Brianna could recognise a baby's cry from five hundred paces, and this baby was in trouble. Big trouble.

'Maybe it's a cat,' Jess observed, following Brianna as she headed back to the consultants' part of the car park. 'Cats and kittens often make a sound like a baby.'

But it wasn't a kitten or a cat. It was a baby who hadn't been there when Brianna had moved her car just a few minutes ago. A baby lying wrapped in a white shawl beside Jess's husband's glossy Aston Martin. A baby whose face was blue, and who was breathing in tiny, rasping gasps.

'Oh, my God!' Jess exclaimed, as Brianna swiftly lifted the tiny bundle into her arms and cradled its head against her breast. 'Who on earth would leave a baby here?'

'It doesn't matter who,' Brianna replied. 'This baby needs attention, and it needs it now.'

She was off and running before Jess could reply. Running so single-mindedly she didn't see the tall figure walking towards her until she almost collided with him.

'Brianna, we need to…' Connor looked down, then up at her incredulously. 'That's a baby.'

'Ten out of ten for observation,' she replied, 'and now can you please get out of my way because it needs help.'

NICU was the obvious place to go, she realised as she ran on with Jess and Connor following her, but she didn't know if the bundle in her arms would make it that far, so she sighed with relief when she saw Josh walking across the entrance foyer of the hospital.

'Hello, gorgeous, where's the fire?' He grinned as she raced towards him.

'No fire,' she replied breathlessly. 'It's a newborn, I found it in the car park, and it's floppy, blue and breathing oddly.'

All Josh's amusement disappeared in a second.

'Jess, can you page Mr Brooke and tell him to come down to A and E immediately? And, if you can't get him,' he added as the counsellor turned to go, 'page Megan. Brianna—you and the baby—A and E—now.'

'My guess is respiratory distress syndrome,' Brianna said as she hurried into A and E and placed the baby on one of the examination tables. 'See how his skin and muscles are being pulled in every time he takes a breath?' she added, carefully unwrapping the shawl. 'How tight his abdomen is?'

'It's a boy?' Connor said, his voice sounding slightly constricted, and Josh frowned at him.

'Who are you?' he demanded. 'The baby's father?'

'I'm Connor Monahan, the hospital auditor.'

'Which doesn't explain why you're here, so I suggest you go and audit something. OK, I wants sats, a ventilator, an umbilical line and a cardio-respiratory monitor,' Josh told his staff. 'And a face mask—the tiniest we've got.'

'BP low, heart rate too high,' one of the A and E nurses declared. 'This baby is going to go into shock if we're not careful.'

'Not on my watch, he won't,' Josh said grimly. 'Where's that umbilical line?'

'Josh, can't you hurry up and stabilise him?' Brianna

said, her eyes fixed anxiously on the baby boy. 'He needs the resources we have in NICU.'

'Agreed, my beautiful colleen,' Josh replied as he began to insert the umbilical line, 'but, as you know very well, stabilising can't be rushed. Poor little mite,' he continued as he checked the cardio-respiratory monitor. 'He can't be more than a couple of days old, which means his mother must need medical attention, too.'

'Yes—yes—whatever,' Brianna said quickly, 'but hurry, Josh, please, hurry.'

'This respiratory distress thing,' Connor said, 'can it be cured?'

Josh looked round at him with irritation.

'Why the hell are you still here? Run out of departments to audit already?'

'I asked a question, and I'd like an answer,' Connor declared, his voice every bit as hard as Josh's, and a small smile curved the A and E consultant's lips.

'Are you quite sure you're not the baby's father? OK—OK,' Josh continued as Brianna threw him an impatient look. 'Yes, Mr Monahan, RDS can be cured. Premature, and very underweight, babies often don't produce enough surfactant in their lungs to help them breathe, but we can give it to them artificially through a breathing tube.'

'But only in NICU,' Megan declared as she swept into A and E, pushing an incubator, 'so can we have a little less chat and a lot more action?'

'I'm simply answering Mr Monahan's question, Megan,' Josh answered mildly, but the paediatric specialist registrar was clearly not about to be placated.

'A question we don't have time for,' she retorted.

'Oh, I always have time for questions,' he countered. 'I don't always give the right answers—'

'Now, there's a surprise—*not*,' Megan replied, her voice cold. 'Perhaps if you spent less time—'

'Look, could the two of you park whatever problem you have with one another and concentrate on this baby?' Brianna exclaimed, then flushed scarlet when she saw Megan's hurt expression and Josh's eyebrows shoot up. 'I'm sorry—I shouldn't have said that—I'm just…'

'Worried.' Josh nodded. 'Understood. OK,' he added as he carefully lifted the baby boy and placed him gently into the incubator, 'this tiny tot is good to go.'

Brianna instantly began pushing the incubator out of A and E towards NICU but it didn't make her feel any better. She'd hurt Megan, she knew she had, and it wasn't as though she hadn't known Megan and Josh had some sort of history so to say what she had…

'Megan, I'm sorry,' she murmured when they reached the unit and Chris began hooking the baby to their monitors. 'What I said—'

'Forget it,' Megan interrupted tightly. 'OK, I want an ultrasound scan, more X-rays and the ophthalmologist.'

'Do you want me to check the sats again?' Brianna said uncertainly. 'Josh's staff did them in A and E, but…'

'Double-check them. Josh's staff aren't specialists, we are.'

'He is going to be all right, isn't he?' Connor asked as he hovered beside them. 'That doctor in A and E—the one who was flirting with Brianna—seemed to think he would be.'

'The doctor's name is Josh O'Hara, and he wasn't flirting with me,' Brianna said swiftly, seeing Megan's head snap up. 'He was just being pleasant.'

'Was he indeed,' Connor murmured dryly, and Brianna could have kicked him for the dark shadow that suddenly appeared in Megan's eyes.

'Look, Connor, why don't you wait outside?' she said abruptly. 'All you're doing is getting in the way.'

'I'll stay,' he said firmly, and, when she turned back to the baby with a shrug, he took a shallow breath.

He couldn't leave, and it wasn't just because he was genuinely concerned about the baby Brianna had found. When she'd almost collided with him outside the hospital he'd been unable to believe what she'd been carrying. The little form so motionless, the shock of thick black hair... For a moment it was as though the last two years had never happened, and then he'd blinked, had seen Brianna's blue uniform, and the two years had rolled back again, bringing with them all the old pain and heartbreak.

He'd told himself that all he wanted from her was answers. He'd told himself she deserved to be punished for what she'd put him through, but he'd seen the pain in her eyes when that A and E consultant had been examining the baby. She was still in her own private hell, just as he was, and lashing out at her wasn't the solution, not if he wanted her back. And he did want her back, he realised, feeling his heart twist inside him as he saw her gently touch the little boy's cheek, because without her... Without her he had nothing.

'Shouldn't the police be alerted?' he said. 'If this baby is only days old, won't his mother need help, too?'

'Good point,' Megan declared. 'Did you see anyone hanging about the car park, Brianna?'

'To be honest, I wasn't looking,' she replied.

In fact, Brianna thought with dawning horror, if Jess hadn't turned up when she had, she would probably have been halfway up the motorway by now, and God knows when this baby would have been found.

'Damn,' Megan muttered. 'Chris, could you try paging Mr Brooke again, see if we can track him down?'

'There's something wrong?' Brianna said, her eyes flying to the baby in the incubator, and Megan shook her head.

'"Wrong" is too strong a word. I'd just be a lot happier if this little chap wasn't quite so inactive. Jess said he was crying when you found him, and yet now...'

'Maybe he's just cold?' Brianna suggested hopefully, and Megan frowned.

'Maybe, but I'd really like Mr Brooke to take a look at this little one. Which reminds me,' she continued, 'we can't keep calling him "little chap" or "little one", until his mother comes forward.'

'How about Patrick?' Chris suggested. 'It's March the seventeenth soon, St Patrick's Day, and you're Irish, Brianna, so I vote we call him Patrick.'

Brianna stared down at the baby boy in the incubator. He was so small, so very small, scarcely 5 pounds in weight, and, gently, she adjusted the pulse oximeter taped to his little foot.

'Harry,' she said softly. 'I'd like...I want to call him Harry.'

She heard Connor's sharp intake of breath, knew what he was thinking, but she didn't turn round, didn't acknowledge him, and Chris shrugged.

'Personally, I still like Patrick, but, as you found him, Brianna, if you want to call him Harry, then Harry he is.'

Just until his mother comes forward, Brianna told herself as she carefully slipped a hat over the baby's head to make sure he didn't lose any more heat. He would only be Harry until his mother claimed him, she knew that, and the mother would come forward, she was sure she would, but until then... Until then she would make sure this little Harry always had someone to care for him, to watch out for him.

It was a very long afternoon. Mr Brooke might eventually have arrived, and announced that in his opinion little Harry was most definitely suffering from respiratory distress syndrome, but he departed again with the observation that he also couldn't rule out the possibility of bronchopulmonary dysplasia.

'Remind me never to be on a sinking ship with that man,' Brianna observed with feeling, and Megan laughed.

'Yeah, he's a regular little ray of sunshine, isn't he?' She glanced down at her watch, and gasped. 'Hey, shouldn't you have been off duty hours ago?'

'I know, I just wanted...' Brianna shrugged helplessly. 'I wanted to stay until I was sure little Harry was OK.'

'Well, in the time-honoured hospital jargon,' Megan replied, 'he's doing as well as can be expected, and to be honest that's about as much as we can expect in the circumstances.'

'How old do you think he is?' Brianna asked, and Megan frowned.

'I'd say a day—two days at most. We're still waiting for the results of the scans to confirm his gestational age, but I don't think he's premature, just very small, which would suggest his mother probably wasn't eating properly.'

'And she's out there somewhere, needing help.' Brianna sighed. 'And I don't have the faintest idea what she looks like. If I'd only kept my wits about me, looked about before I rushed her son into the hospital...'

'Hey, don't beat yourself up over it—Jess didn't see anyone either,' Megan replied, then glanced over her shoulder and lowered her voice. 'How's it going with Connor?'

Brianna grimaced. 'What do you think?'

'At least he seems to have finally left for the day,' Megan observed, 'or maybe he's just annoying the hell out of the staff in some other department. Whichever it is, I'd cut and run if I were you. And, yes, I'll phone you at home if there's any change in Harry,' she continued as Brianna made to interrupt, 'so go, will you?'

Brianna laughed and nodded, but, as she turned to leave, she paused.

'Megan, what I said this afternoon in A and E… If I could take it back, I would. If I could reverse the clock, I'd do it in a minute. What I said was so thoughtless—'

'But correct,' the paediatric specialist registrar interrupted. 'Josh and I should have been concentrating on little Harry. It's just… I'm afraid the two of us only have to be in the same room together now and…' She smiled a little unevenly. 'Let's just say it's not good.'

Brianna knew exactly what Megan meant as she left the unit and drove home, but the trouble was she didn't even have to be in the same room with Connor for her nerves to be on edge. Even when she got home to her cottage in the small fishing village of Penhally, and had changed into a pair of jeans and a sweatshirt, she couldn't relax, couldn't stop thinking about him.

Diversion, she thought as she picked up a book, only to just as quickly discard it. If she'd reached home at her normal time she would have gone for a walk on the beach to try to calm herself, but it was too dark for that now. What she needed was something—or someone—to channel her thoughts elsewhere, so, when her doorbell rang, a little after nine o'clock, she hastened to answer it. With luck it might be Jess who sometimes stopped by to discuss how the parents of a baby in NICU were—or weren't—coping, and they could have a cup of coffee, and chat, but it wasn't Jess on her doorstep, it was Connor.

'If you're here to talk to me about the unit,' she said quickly, 'it's late, it's been a long day, and I'm tired.'

'I haven't come to talk to you about the unit,' he replied, putting out his hand to stop her as she began to close the door on him. 'I've come to see you.'

And he had a suitcase with him, she noticed with dawning dismay. A suitcase that could only mean one thing.

'Connor, you can't think…' She dragged her gaze away from the suitcase, and back to him. 'You're not expecting to move in here with me, are you?'

'I figured it was stupid to keep staying in a hotel when you have a house within easy driving distance of St Piran, so I checked out of my hotel this evening.'

'But you can't,' she protested. 'People will talk. They'll say—'

'That a husband is living with his wife?' he suggested, and she flushed, and regrouped hurriedly.

'But won't your impartiality be compromised if you stay with me?' she exclaimed. 'I know you would never shut down an NICU but people could think—might suggest—I had exerted undue influence upon your report.'

'Then people would be wrong, wouldn't they?' he replied smoothly. 'So, are you going to leave me standing on the doorstep, or let me in?'

He'd backed her into a corner. Her only way out would be to tell him the truth, that she didn't want him in her home, prodding and poking at old wounds, but though he had asked her for honesty she knew she couldn't be quite that honest with him.

'You'd better come in,' she said in defeat.

'Nice house,' he observed as he followed her down the

narrow hallway into her sitting room, having to duck to avoid hitting his head on the old oak beams across the ceiling. 'Very…compact.'

'Tiny, you mean,' she said. 'I suppose it is, but I like it.'

'And this is where you've been living for the last two years?' he said, putting his suitcase down by the coffee table, and she nodded.

'I lived in nurses' accommodation at the hospital for a few weeks when I first came to Cornwall, but I wanted somewhere to call home so I rented this.'

'You have a home,' he reminded her, 'in London. Our flat.'

But it isn't mine, she thought. It never was mine, but I don't think I'll ever get you to understand that.

'Would you like something to eat?' she said, deliberately changing the subject. 'I was just about to raid my kitchen.'

'That would be nice.'

She didn't know if it would be nice, but eating something would certainly be preferable to them simply staring at one another in awkward silence for the rest of the evening, or, even worse, talking about things she didn't want to talk about.

'Chilli, lasagne or beef casserole?' she asked as she went into the kitchen and opened the freezer.

'Lasagne was always my favourite.'

It had been. She couldn't recall how many times she'd made it for him in the past but that had been then, this was now.

'Lasagne it is,' she said, and, as she placed it in the microwave, she prayed he would eat it quickly so she could retreat to the safety of her bedroom.

But he didn't eat quickly. In fact, he seemed to be in no hurry at all.

'This is lovely,' he declared as he forked some lasagne into his mouth. 'Every bit as good as I remember.'

'I'm glad,' she said, pushing her own lasagne around the plate without enthusiasm. 'Would you like some wine to go with your meal?' she continued, half rising to her feet, only to sit down again as he shook his head. 'Connor…' *Get it out,* she thought, *just say it.* 'Why have you really come?'

'Because we need to talk, and there's never any opportunity at the hospital.'

Which was fair enough, but that didn't mean she had to like it.

'That doctor at the hospital,' he continued, 'the A and E one who was flirting with you—'

'How many times do I have to tell you he wasn't flirting with me?' she interrupted with a huff of impatience. 'Josh is from Ireland, as you and I are, and the way he talks… It's just his style. He does it with every woman he meets, whether she's nine or ninety. And anyway,' she added for good measure, 'he's married.'

'So are you,' Connor observed, staring pointedly at her left hand, 'and yet you're not wearing your wedding ring.'

Damn, she'd forgotten about that, and she felt a warm flush of colour creep across her cheeks.

'I took it off when I came here,' she said uncomfortably. 'I thought…I felt it would be easier, would mean I wouldn't have to explain anything, or answer any awkward questions.'

'And is that what I am for you now—an awkwardness?' he said, putting down his knife and fork. 'Someone it's better not to think about, someone who can be jettisoned as easily as pulling off a ring?'

She could see the hurt in his blue eyes, but what could she say? Wasn't that exactly how she regarded his reappearance in her life? As something she'd far rather not deal with, someone she wished hadn't reappeared? And yet the man sitting in front of her was her husband, the man she had once pledged to love for the rest of her life.

'Connor, I know you want answers—and you're entitled to them,' she said unhappily, 'but I can't deal with this right now. I'm sorry—'

'You keep saying that as though it somehow makes everything all right,' he retorted, and she bit her lip.

'I know it doesn't make everything all right. I know it's not enough, but…' She took a breath, and it sounded unsteady even to her own ears. 'Can't you see this is hard for me?'

'And you think it's easy for me?' he exclaimed. 'Easy for me to sit at a table with my wife, knowing she doesn't want me here? Easy for me, today in the unit, when you named that baby Harry? You should never have done that, Brianna, *never.*'

She stretched out her hand to him, half in apology, half in a plea for understanding, but he pulled away from her.

'Connor, he hasn't got anyone, not right now,' she said with difficulty. 'He's all alone, and he…he's so very little, so fragile, and he reminded me so much of our son.'

'But he isn't our son,' he retorted, pain clear in his eyes. 'He isn't our Harry, Brianna.'

'I know,' she said. 'I know he has a mother, that she'll come back for him eventually, but until then—'

'You can pretend he's Harry?' he finished for her, his eyes fixed on her, daring her to contradict him. 'You can pretend we didn't lose our son—is that what you're saying?'

'No— Yes—' She shook her head. 'I don't know. All I know is this baby needs me right now, Connor.'

'*I* need you!' he exclaimed. 'I'm here, and *I* need you.'

'But when I needed you, you weren't there for me,' she blurted out, and saw his face contort with disbelief.

'How can you say that?' he demanded. 'I was always there for you, and our son. *Always!*'

'Not enough to let me cry for him after he died,' she threw back at him. 'Whenever I cried you'd say, "Don't cry, Brianna. You mustn't cry."'

'You were making yourself ill—'

'And whenever I tried to talk about him you changed the subject. My parents—my friends—because Harry died twelve hours after he was born—they never saw him, so he wasn't…' She swallowed hard. 'He wasn't real to them. They had no memories of him, only you and I did, but you… You just seemed to want to airbrush him out of our lives.'

'That is an unforgivable thing to say,' he replied, his voice raw. 'He was my son, too.'

'A son you would never talk about—a son you never cried over!'

'Brianna, if talking would have brought Harry back, I would have talked myself hoarse,' he protested, 'but talking wouldn't have changed anything, you know it wouldn't.'

'It would have kept him alive for me,' she said, tears thickening her voice. 'It would have kept him alive, and with us, but you… It was like you'd decided it was better to pretend he'd never lived, had never been.'

'Brianna—'

'All through the funeral you just sat there as though what was happening…what the priest was saying…was nothing to do with you while I… I kept thinking he'll wake up, Harry's going to wake up, and cry, and they'll realise they've made a mistake, and then I can take him home, and I so…' She let out a small sob. 'I so wanted to take him home.'

'Brianna, please—'

'You want to know how I really felt before I left you?' she continued, dashing a hand across her eyes. 'I wanted to die, Connor. All I wanted was to die, so I could be with Harry, and then he…' Her voice broke. 'He wouldn't be alone, and I couldn't bear the thought of him being alone, in the dark, with no one to hold him.'

'Brianna, *don't*,' he said, his voice cracking. 'Please, *don't*.'

'See—you're doing it again,' she cried. 'You say you want us to talk, but every time I try, you cut me off.'

'Because I can't bear to see you upset,' he said hoarsely. 'I can't bear to see you suffer like this.'

'Connor—'

'You're right,' he said, abruptly getting to his feet. 'It's been a long day, and we're both tired, and I still need to unpack.'

His face was closed and tight. It was the expression she'd grown used to seeing before she'd left him. The one that told her he didn't want to listen to her, didn't want to hear what she was saying, and she stood up, too, in defeat.

'What about the dishes?' he continued as she walked past him towards the kitchen door. 'You could wash, and I could dry, just like we used to.'

'Leave them,' she muttered. 'I'll do them later.'

'But—'

But nothing, she thought, walking determinedly into the sitting room, then up the narrow staircase to the first floor, leaving him with nothing to do but follow her. She didn't want to play happy couples with him in the kitchen, pretending that everything was all right over the washing-up. They weren't a happy couple. They hadn't been one for a very long time.

'The bathroom's in here,' she said as she opened the first door on the landing. 'It has both a bath and a shower so you can have whichever you want.'

'Looks good,' he replied with a smile, which she didn't return.

'I hope you'll be comfortable in here,' she said, walking into the next room. 'There's a double bed so you shouldn't feel cramped, and plenty of hanging space for your clothes—'

'But it's not your room.'

It was a statement, not a question, and she smoothed down the duvet, which didn't need smoothing, and deliberately avoided his eyes.

'The room faces south so you'll get the sun in the morning,' she continued, 'and there's a lovely view of Penhally bay and the harbour—'

'Brianna, when I said I needed you, I meant every word.'

His voice was soft, entreating, and she forced herself to look up at him. He was the man she had married, the man she'd fallen in love with all those years ago, and yet now... She knew she should feel something, ought to feel something, but it was as though her heart was frozen, and where there should have been love for him there was nothing but pain.

'Connor, I can't just go back to the way we were before Harry died,' she said haltingly. 'I can't pretend everything's all right between us, or forget, or—'

'Share my bed.'

She shook her head, unable to speak.

'Would…?' He took a deep breath. 'Would you rather I just left?'

'Yes' would have been her honest answer, but she knew she couldn't say that. She'd accused him of never talking, of never telling her what he was thinking and maybe, if he stayed, maybe he might talk, maybe he might listen, and she had to at least give him that opportunity.

'You have every right to be here,' she said.

Which wasn't what he wanted to hear, he thought as she left the room. He didn't want to hear he had a 'right' to be there by virtue of being her husband. He wanted her to say she wanted him there, but she hadn't.

Why had he come? he wondered as he sat down heavily on the bed. He should never have come, except…

He'd told himself he wanted answers. He still wanted them, but he wanted more than that. He didn't want to lose her, not again. He didn't want her to just slip away from him, and she was slipping away, he knew she was.

With a sigh he stood up and walked over to the window and gazed out. It was too cloudy tonight for stars, but he could see a light in the distance. A light that went on and off rhythmically. A lighthouse, his brain registered. A lighthouse, which gave hope to sailors lost at sea, and hope was all he had right now. A hope that was much fainter than the lighthouse's bright beam, but he would hold onto it because there was nothing else he could do.

CHAPTER THREE

'I JUST wish I could have been more help to the police yesterday,' Brianna said as she checked the cardio monitor above Amy Renwick's incubator. 'They were so kind, so patient—even offered to bring in their face-imaging expert, to see if I could re-create an image of Harry's mother—but I honestly and truly don't remember seeing anyone in the car park.'

'Neither did Sid, or Jess, so you're not the only one,' Megan said soothingly. 'Have the police had any luck identifying where Harry's shawl might have been bought?'

Brianna shook her head.

'Apparently it can be bought in lots of high-street shops, which means the mother could have come from anywhere.'

'She'll be some local, unmarried teenager.' Rita sniffed as she appeared, clutching a sheaf of forms. 'You know the sort—the airhead kind who think having a baby will be fun until they're presented with the reality. I'd wager my next pay cheque we'll never see her again.'

'Of course we'll see her,' Brianna said, hearing Megan's sharp intake of breath. 'She'll realise she's made a mistake, and come forward to claim her son. What mother wouldn't?'

'The irresponsible sort,' Rita declared. 'The sort whose

families have never given them any proper values, or a decent upbringing. *My* daughters waited until they had a wedding ring on their finger before they hopped into bed with the first man who paid them any attention.'

'Girls—women—become pregnant for all sorts of reasons,' Brianna said stiffly, 'and I don't think we—as medical staff—should set ourselves up as either judge or jury.'

'Too right,' Megan said, her voice ice-cold. 'Are those forms for me?' she continued, gazing pointedly at the papers in Rita's hand.

'They're admission slips for the babies who came in last night,' the ward clerk replied. 'You have to sign them in triplicate.'

'Bureaucracy gone mad,' Megan muttered. 'What's the stats for the new admissions?'

'Both full term,' Brianna replied. 'One has severe jaundice, the other congenital hypothyroidism. Mr Brooke started the jaundiced baby on phototherapy last night, and the CH baby is being given oral thyroid hormone.'

'Good.' Megan nodded, then frowned as she gazed out over the ward. 'Unfortunately that means we're now at full capacity, so let's hope we don't get hit by another emergency admission.'

'And that would be a problem?'

Connor had joined them, his phone poised and ready in his hand, and Brianna gritted her teeth at the sight of it, and him.

'We have six incubators, which now have six babies in them,' she replied. 'Do the maths, Connor.'

'I can count as well as you can,' he replied mildly, 'but I understood you had an arrangement with the hospital in Plymouth to take any babies you were unable to admit?'

Out of the corner of her eye, Brianna could see Megan

determinedly shepherding Rita towards the ward door, but she didn't give a damn whether Rita stayed and eaves-dropped or not.

'We do,' she declared, 'but, as I explained to you yesterday—though you clearly weren't listening—sending babies so far from their homes is upsetting for everyone.'

'I hardly think a thirty—or thirty-five—minute drive could be considered particularly stressful,' Connor observed, and Brianna gritted her teeth until they hurt.

'I wonder how stress-free you'd find that journey if you received a phone call in the middle of the night telling you your baby's condition had deteriorated?' she demanded. 'Or how stress-free you'd be if you arrived to discover your son, or daughter, had died? Not all babies leave NICU alive, Connor.' She met his gaze. 'You should know that.'

It had been a low blow, and she knew it, as she saw all colour drain from his face, but she'd had enough of him today. If she was going to be honest, she'd had more than enough of him by the time they'd shared an excruciatingly awkward breakfast in her home this morning, and the last thing she needed was him dogging her every step, making stupid comments.

'Sister Flannigan?'

Brianna glanced over her shoulder to see Naomi Renwick hovering uncertainly by the ward door, clearly unsure as to whether she should approach or not, and hitched a smile to her lips.

'What can I do for you, Naomi?'

'Nothing, really. It's just...' Amy's mother flushed. 'Experience has taught me that if more than one person is clustered round my daughter's incubator, something's wrong.'

'Far from it,' Brianna insisted. 'I completed Amy's obs about half an hour ago, and there was no sign of any post-op infection, and her sats are perfect. Of course, we're going to have to wait and see what happens when we start feeding her orally instead of through an IV line, but at the moment I'd say everything's looking pretty good.'

'Thank you, Sister, thank you so much,' Naomi said, letting out the breath Brianna knew she'd been holding. 'I know it's silly to always suspect the worst, but sometimes—'

'It seems as though all you've done, since Amy was born, is take one step forward and two steps back,' Brianna finished for her. 'I do understand, but try not to worry, OK?'

'I'll try,' Naomi promised, and, when Brianna hurried across the ward in answer to Megan's beckoning wave, she smiled up at Connor. 'Sister Flannigan is always so encouraging, isn't she?'

'She would appear to be,' he replied noncommittally.

'Are you a doctor, Mr…Mr…?'

'Monahan. Connor Monahan,' he said, 'and, no, I'm not a doctor. I'm…' His lips curved a little ruefully. 'I guess you could call me a glorified accountant.'

'Right.' Naomi nodded, clearly none the wiser. 'This is my daughter, Amy,' she continued, gently touching the incubator. 'She was born two months premature.'

And I don't want to know this, Connor thought, half turning to go, but Mrs Renwick wasn't finished.

'All the nursing staff here are really wonderful,' she continued, 'but Sister Flannigan… She's something special, you know?'

He did know, he thought as he noticed Brianna's brow begin to furrow at whatever Megan was saying. He'd known it from the very first moment they'd met, when he'd been twenty-two, and Brianna had been twenty-one. All it had taken was one shy smile from her, across the dance floor in her home town of Killarney, and he'd fallen for her completely.

'It's like she somehow knows how all we parents feel,' Naomi observed. 'That she's not simply mouthing words of sympathy, but really understands what it's like to worry, and to fear.'

They had both known worry, and fear, Connor thought, feeling his stomach clench as memories surfaced in his mind, memories which were as bitter as they were unwanted. When Harry had been born, one month early, he'd known so little, been so naive. What's a month? he had asked himself. Babies of less than twenty-eight weeks survived, so a one-month-early baby was nothing, but then the hospital consultant had dropped his bombshell.

'Everyone says Mr Brooke is an excellent surgeon,' Naomi continued, 'and I'm sure he is, but he is a little...a little...'

'Brusque?' Connor suggested, and Naomi chuckled.

'Downright depressing would be closer to the truth. I know he has to be honest, but...'

'You'd prefer a little less honesty, and a bit more hope?'

Naomi nodded. 'Dr Phillips is always very upbeat— she's nice, too. In fact, I'm surprised a pretty woman like her isn't married, but then neither is Sister Flannigan, and I think she's just lovely.'

She was, Connor thought, glancing across the ward at Brianna. With hair the colour of burnished autumn leaves, large brown eyes and a smile that had always made his heart beat faster, she looked again like the girl he had married ten years ago rather than the skeletally thin woman who had left him. Over and over again he had begged and pleaded with her to eat, but she'd simply stared back at him with eyes that seemed to have grown too big for her small face. Now she'd regained some of the weight she'd lost, and he could not help but wonder what—or who—had finally persuaded her to eat.

'I understand… Sister Flannigan…I believe she's quite close to that A and E doctor—Josh O'Hara?' Connor commented, despising himself for asking, but needing to know nevertheless.

'Oh, no,' Naomi replied. 'He does come into the unit occasionally, and he certainly makes her laugh, but he's married, and, even if he wasn't, I wouldn't say he was Sister Flannigan's type.'

'You wouldn't?' Connor said hopefully, and Naomi shook her head.

'If you want my opinion, I'd say Dr O'Hara and Dr Phillips would be better suited. They just sort of look right together, if you know what I mean, though, of course, people do say it's often opposites who attract.'

Everyone in Killarney had wondered what Brianna had seen in him, Connor recalled wryly—she with her gift of always being able to talk to anyone, and he so very reserved unless he was discussing a balance sheet—but they'd been happy, they'd loved one another, and then Harry had been born.

'It's so sad about Harry.'

Connor's eyes shot to Mrs Renwick, wondering for one awful moment if she could possibly have read his mind, but she wasn't talking about his son. She was gazing at the incubator nearest the wall, and his forehead creased with foreboding.

'His condition has worsened?'

'Oh, no—at least, I don't think it has,' Mrs Renwick said quickly. 'I meant it's very sad that his mother abandoned him like that, but at least he's got Sister Flannigan.'

And Connor wished the child hadn't as he watched

Brianna walk away from Megan to the little boy's incubator. God knows, he meant the child no harm but, after just one day of looking after him, he knew Brianna was getting too close, and if this child died…

He closed his eyes tightly, but it didn't help. Nothing would ever erase the memory of that day when they'd come home from the hospital, after it was all over. Never had he heard anyone cry the way Brianna had cried, like an animal racked with pain, and he never wanted to hear that sound again, but the longer this baby's mother didn't come forward the more involved Brianna would become, and all he could see was heartbreak ahead for her no matter what happened.

'Are you all right, Mr Monahan?'

He opened his eyes to see Naomi gazing up at him with concern, and manufactured a smile.

'I'm fine. It's just…wards like this… You never know what's going to happen next, and I find that…unsettling.'

'My husband's the same.' Naomi nodded. 'He likes certainty, too, but I keep telling him, think positive, it's the only thing you can do.'

And Connor was positive something had just gone very wrong as he saw Megan join Brianna at Harry's incubator, and his wife begin to shake her head angrily.

'I'm afraid you'll have to excuse me, Mrs Renwick…'

He was vaguely aware that Amy's mother said something in reply, but he couldn't have said what. His eyes were fixed on Brianna. She looked upset now as well as angry, and whether she wanted him at her side was immaterial. He was going to be there.

'Problem?' he said as he approached her, and saw Megan bite her lip.

'There's a reporter outside in the corridor from the *Penhally Gazette*,' the paediatric specialist registrar replied.

'He wants to interview Brianna for his newspaper, and
Admin think it would be an excellent way to give Harry
more exposure, and perhaps encourage his mother to come
forward.'

'And Admin can whistle Dixie as far as I'm concerned
because I know damn fine that the only exposure Vermin
would give Harry is the muckraking kind,' Brianna said
tartly.

'Vermin?' Connor echoed, his eyebrows rising.

'His actual name is Kennie Vernon,' Megan replied, 'but
he's known as Vermin for a very good reason. Not only
does he work on the principle of never letting the truth get
in the way of a good story, he's also the man who told the
world—or at least the St Piran and Penhally part of it—that
Jess has—'

The paediatric specialist registrar came to a sudden,
red-cheeked halt, clearly deeply mortified by what she had
almost said, and Connor glanced from her to Brianna, his
eyebrows raised.

'Jess Corezzi has what?' he asked, and saw Brianna
grimace.

'She has HIV, Connor,' she said in a low undertone.
'And before you say anything—'

'All I was going to say was, so what?' he replied, and
Brianna sighed.

'Unfortunately that wasn't most people's reaction when
Vernon splashed her condition all over the front page of
the *Penhally Gazette*. I will never, ever forgive him for the
way he crucified her, Connor, and for Admin to think I'd
be willing to even be in the same room as that man, far
less give him an interview…'

'Look, would it help if I sat in with you?' he said. 'I
wouldn't interfere, I promise I wouldn't,' he added as
Brianna began to shake her head, 'but I do have a lot of

experience in dealing with the press through my work, and, whether you like it or not, Admin is right. The more press exposure the hospital can generate about this baby, the better.'

Megan caught Brianna's gaze.

'He's right,' she said reluctantly. 'I know you don't want to do it—I wouldn't want to either—but if Connor is there as back-up…?'

'I don't need back-up,' Brianna said, annoyance plain in her voice. 'I'm a big girl. I don't need my hand held.'

'No one is suggesting you do,' Connor said gently. 'But don't ever underestimate the press, Brianna, and sometimes two heads are better than one when it comes to dealing with the enemy.'

For a moment Brianna said nothing, then she let out a small, grudging sigh.

'OK. All right. I'll do it. Where is the little toad?'

Megan grinned.

'I told him to wait outside in the corridor. I also made him thoroughly scrub and disinfect his hands. He wasn't very happy about either.'

'Good,' Brianna declared. 'OK, Connor, let's you and I go and slaughter the little jumped-up slimeball.'

Wrong, Brianna, Connor thought as he followed her out of the ward and he saw the man waiting for them at the end of the corridor. Kennie Vernon might look like a refugee from a very bad eighties pop video, with his goatee beard and ponytail, but the muddy brown eyes that watched them walking towards him were calculating and shrewd. This was not a man to underestimate. This was a man who would use anyone, and anything, to get himself out of the *Penhally Gazette* and into one of the big London newspapers, and Connor instinctively moved closed to his wife.

'Sister Flannigan,' Kennie declared with a smile that

was every bit as false as the replica Rolex on his wrist. 'How very pleasant to meet you.'

'I'm afraid I can't the say the same,' she replied. 'I'm not that big a hypocrite.'

Kennie's smile didn't slip at all as he transferred his gaze to Connor.

'And you are…?'

'He's…' Brianna came to a dead halt. How on earth was she supposed to introduce Connor? If she said he was her husband, Vermin would dig deeper, and if she said Connor was an auditor, that would give the reporter an even bigger story for the *Penhally Gazette*. 'He's—'

'Connor Monahan. Sister Flannigan's PR adviser,' Connor announced, and it wasn't only Brianna's jaw that dropped.

'You have a public relations adviser?' Kennie said to Brianna, but again it was Connor who answered.

'Naturally,' he said, in a tone that suggested only complete losers didn't. 'Now, I'm sure you don't want to conduct this interview in a corridor,' he continued, 'so shall we adjourn to my office?'

He opened the door of the nurse unit manager's office pointedly, and Kennie Vernon walked into it without a word, but as Connor made to follow him, Brianna caught hold of his arm.

'Why the hell did you say that?' she hissed. 'About you being my PR adviser?'

Connor shrugged. 'I had a sort of flash of inspiration.'

'Yeah, right,' she replied. 'Well, try not to have too many more of them, OK?'

And he smiled. A smile that made her heart clench because it suddenly transported her right back to that night in Killarney when her eyes had met his over the crowded dance floor. She'd known immediately that he wasn't local, and so had all the other girls.

'He's here on holiday,' someone had whispered. 'From Dublin.'

And her friends had all giggled, and nudged one another, because, to them, Dublin was somewhere exotic, somewhere exciting. He'd looked so out of place in the village hall, dressed in his crisp white shirt, blue tie and smart black trousers, while all the other young men had been wearing jeans and T-shirts, but when he hadn't reacted to her friends' giggles, or their fluttering eyelashes, they'd all muttered, 'Stuck-up prat,' and dismissed him, but she'd hadn't.

She'd kept sneaking curious glances at him, and his eyes had eventually met hers, and he'd smiled. The same half crooked, half self-deprecating, smile he was smiling now, and she hadn't seen that smile in such a long time.

'What?' he asked as she stared up at him, and she shook her head.

'Nothing. It's…nothing.'

But it was, she thought as she went into the nurse unit manager's office. It was a painful reminder of how she'd once felt about the man at her side. A bitter-sweet reminder that she'd once loved him more than life, and had thought nothing would ever separate them.

'I understand Jessica Corezzi was with you when you found this baby?' Kennie declared, sitting down and instantly flipping open his notebook, pen poised.

'Yes, she was,' Brianna replied, deliberately remaining standing.

'She married a consultant at the hospital recently, didn't she?' Kennie murmured. 'Which is somewhat surprising given the circumstances.'

Because Jess has HIV, Brianna thought angrily. That's

what you're saying, you horrible little man. That you're amazed she could actually find someone willing to marry her, and she wasn't about to let him get away with that.

'Now, just one minute,' she began, only to pause when Connor shook his head warningly at her.

'Both Jess Corezzi and Sister Flannigan found the baby together,' Connor said smoothly, 'but, unfortunately, neither of them saw the mother. Or the father, come to that,' he added with a smile. 'After all, why be sexist, why assume it was the mother who left the baby there?'

'Right.' Kennie Vernon nodded, looking slightly bemused, but he wasn't finished. Not by a long shot. 'It's strange, don't you think, Sister Flannigan, that the baby should be found in the consultants' car park?'

'Strange?' she repeated, puzzled. 'I'm sorry, but I don't understand what you mean.'

'I was just wondering whether the unfortunate mother might perhaps have had a relationship with one of the consultants in the hospital,' Kennie said, 'and she left the baby where he would find it because he'd dumped her.'

And you know exactly whose car little Harry was found next to, Brianna thought furiously. It was Gio Corezzi's car. Jess's husband.

'Mr Vernon,' she began, but Connor cut across her again.

'I fear you may have been reading far too many trashy novelettes, Mr Vernon,' he drawled. 'Surely the most plausible explanation is that the mother left her baby in that particular car park because it was the furthest from the road and she wanted to ensure her child didn't become…' He frowned in apparent concentration. 'Now, what's the word I'm looking for… Ah, yes. Road kill.'

Road kill? Brianna thought, shooting her husband an

appalled glance, and could almost have sworn she saw him wink back at her.

'I think the term you were searching for, Mr Monahan, is road fatality,' Kennie Vernon said stiffly, then flipped over a page of his notebook. 'Colour of hair and eyes of this child, and does he have any distinguishing features like a birthmark or a mole?'

'Harry has black hair, and blue eyes,' Brianna replied, 'but no birthmarks or moles.'

'Harry?'

'We didn't want to keep calling him Baby X,' Brianna replied uncomfortably, 'so we decided to name him Harry until his mother comes forward.'

'I'd like to take a photograph—'

'No, absolutely not,' Brianna interrupted. 'I can take a photograph of him for your newspaper if you want one, but I cannot allow you into the ward because of the risk of infection.'

Kennie leant back in his seat, and smiled at her with a smile she did not care for.

'Are you always this obstructive, Sister Flannigan?' he asked, and she saw Connor move forward a step.

'Sister Flannigan is merely stating hospital policy,' her husband replied in a tone that suggested arguing would be most unwise, but that did not prevent the reporter from trying.

'I'd like to remind both of you of the rights of the press—'

'Which I do not think would ever include endangering the life of a very vulnerable baby,' Connor declared.

'But—'

'You could, of course, apply for a court order,' Connor continued smoothly, 'but I think that would be…unwise.

Unless you wish to be front-page news yourself for harassing a minor?'

Kennie shot Connor a look that was positively venomous, then snapped his notebook shut.

'Thank you for your time,' he said as he stood up. 'That will be all.'

'No, it won't.' Brianna sighed as the reporter strode out the office without a backward glance. 'He'll be back.'

'Undoubtedly,' Connor agreed. 'But round one to us, I think.'

'I'm just very glad you were on my side,' Brianna said with feeling, and Connor smiled, a slightly lopsided smile.

'I always was, I always will be,' he said simply.

There was no answer to that except one, which she knew would hurt him immeasurably, so she opted to change the subject.

'Road kill, Connor?' she said as she led the way into the corridor. *'Road kill?'*

'I had a momentary memory lapse, couldn't remember the correct phrase.' He grinned, and she shook her head at him and chuckled.

'Yeah, right,' she said. 'And like I would ever believe that. You never forget anything.'

'Except, it seems, the things that really matter,' he murmured.

His eyes were troubled, but what could she say to him when she knew he'd spoken the truth?

'Have you seen our graduation board?' she asked, trying to change the subject.

'Your what?' he said with an effort, and she pointed to the board on the corridor wall, which was covered with baby pictures.

'It started shortly after the unit was opened,' she said.

'Parents of babies who had left the unit, gone home, began putting up pictures of their children to give other parents encouragement, to let them see there was light at the end of the tunnel, and it sort of snowballed.'

He grimaced slightly. 'I see. Brianna—'

'Hands,' she said. 'If you're going back into the ward you need to thoroughly scrub and disinfect your hands.'

'Oh. Right. Sorry,' he replied, but after he'd thoroughly scrubbed his hands, and she had, too, he turned to her uncertainly. 'How can you bear to work here after losing Harry? Don't you find it incredibly stressful to be constantly surrounded by very ill babies?'

'It can certainly be challenging, and upsetting at times,' she agreed as she pushed open the ward door, 'but…you see…with Harry…' She took a steadying breath. 'There was nothing I could do, nothing anyone would let me do, but working as a nurse in here, I know there are times when I can make a difference, times when my skills matter, and I can help.'

'Yes, but even so, don't you—?'

'Oh, *hell.*'

For a second, Connor was completely bewildered by her exclamation, but as he looked past her, into the ward, he saw what she had. Megan was standing at the top of the ward, her eyes fixed firmly on one of the monitors, while Josh was ostensibly deeply in conversation with Mr Brooke, but only a fool wouldn't have noticed that the A and E consultant's eyes kept darting in the direction of the paediatric specialist registrar.

'What gives between those two?' Connor asked in an undertone. 'Every time they meet I swear Megan's back couldn't get any stiffer if she had a poker strapped to it, and yet Josh constantly seems to be trying to gain her attention.'

'It's none of my business,' Brianna replied firmly, 'or yours.'

'Fair point,' Connor conceded, 'but it's odd.'

It *was* odd, Brianna thought as Mr Brooke bore Connor off to interview some of the nurses in Gynae, and she saw Josh make an attempt to talk to Megan, an attempt she very quickly rebuffed. Normally, Josh didn't seek Megan out. They might occasionally meet because of their work, but he had never actively attempted to get her to talk to him so this was different, and puzzling.

'You OK?' she said to Megan when Josh finally left.

The paediatric specialist registrar faked a smile.

'Shouldn't that be my question?' she said. 'After all, you were the one who was being interviewed by horrible Vermin, so how did it go?'

Which was as neat a way as any of avoiding answering, Brianna thought, but who was she to point the finger?

'He was his usual obnoxious self,' she said, 'but Connor took no prisoners.'

Megan nodded.

'Connor…' she began carefully '…he seems…nice. Maybe a bit of a statistic obsessive—'

'A bit?'

'OK, a lot,' Megan agreed with a small chuckle, then her face grew serious. 'Look, Brianna, I guess, what I'm trying to say—very badly—is, if you want to—you know—talk at any time, I'm a good listener.'

'Me, too, if you ever want to talk—you know—about Josh,' Brianna replied.

'Yeah, well, Josh and I…' Megan gave a dismissive smile that didn't fool Brianna for a second. 'That ship sailed a long time ago.'

Had Connor and her ship sailed, too? Brianna wondered as the rest of the day sped by in a round of obs, X-rays and scans. She didn't know, but neither did she want to answer the other question of whether she actually wanted to still be on board.

But it was a question that wasn't going to go away, she realised when her shift ended, and she drove home to find Connor's Range Rover already parked outside her house. It was a question she was ultimately going to have to face, but not now, she decided as she got out of her car, grabbed her jacket, and determinedly took the rocky path that led down to the beach.

Except the walk had been a very bad idea, she realised when she reached the shore and recognised a familiar figure standing there, gazing out to sea. A figure who saw her just as soon as she saw him, giving her no chance to slip away.

'I thought I'd get some air,' he said as she slowly walked towards him.

'Me, too,' she replied. 'I often walk here after work. I find it helps if…' She had been going to say, 'If I'm stressed,' but that didn't seem the kindest thing to say in the circumstances. 'I find it clears away the cobwebs.'

A bracing March wind was blowing across the beach, whipping the slate-grey sea into frothy white breakers, and sending dark clouds scudding across the sky, and Connor smiled wryly.

'I can believe that,' he said, and an involuntary chuckle broke from her.

'You hate it here, don't you?'

'Not hate, exactly,' he replied as she began walking along the beach, and he fell into step beside her, 'but…' He waved his hand towards the small cottages dotted along the hillside, the rows of houses nestling further down around the bay that made up the town of Penhally. 'Don't you find it incredibly claustrophobic? All those net curtains constantly twitching, the way everyone knows everyone else's business, and what they don't know they make up?'

'People can only know what you choose to tell them,' she replied. 'For sure they can speculate, gossip, but you'll find gossips everywhere.'

'But Penhally—and St Piran—they're both so far from civilisation,' he insisted, and she smiled.

'When I first came here I heard a holidaymaker say that to one of the old fishermen, and he said, "It all depends on what you mean by 'civilisation'". Of course we don't have big shops, and there's no cinema, or any sort of nightclub, but if you need help it's always given. Actually, it reminds me a lot of home.'

'But it's nothing like London,' he protested, and she blinked.

'I meant Killarney. London was never my home.'

'Brianna, we lived in London for nine years,' he replied with ill-disguised irritation. 'It was most definitely our home.'

'Maybe for you,' she muttered, but he heard her, and came to a halt, forcing her to stop, too.

'All right, explain,' he demanded, and she opened her mouth, then closed it again to marshal her thoughts.

'Do you remember the flat we rented in Killarney when we first got married?' she said, and he groaned.

'Do I ever? It was so small, and dingy, and whenever I had a bath every damn pipe in the place rattled.'

'OK,' she conceded, with a small gurgle of laughter, 'so the plumbing wasn't the greatest—'

'And the mice...' He rolled his eyes heavenwards. 'Brianna, the place was overrun with mice, and you'd never let me kill any of them so I was constantly catching them in those humane boxes, and taking them outside, until Mr Fitzgerald told us that unless I took them at least six miles away they'd find their own way back.'

'So you used to load up the car every weekend, and drive them out to the country,' she chuckled, remembering, and he shook his head ruefully.

'A proper eejit I looked, too, emptying all of those boxes into a field like some sort of Pied Piper.'

And his Irish accent was coming back, she noticed, the accent he had so carefully excised from his voice because he didn't want to be thought provincial by all the big shots in London.

'And don't forget Mrs O'Leary in the flat next door,' he continued. 'Always wanting to tell us how much the flats had gone downhill since her husband died, and that bright red wig she wore—'

'Oh, I'd forgotten all about her wig,' Brianna declared, starting to laugh, 'and her hats—do you remember the hats she used to wear—all those feathers, and ribbons, and bows?'

'Brianna, I swear those hats will remain scarred on my psyche for ever,' Connor said with a shudder.

And she laughed out loud, and it was so good to hear her laugh, had been so long since he'd heard her laugh, and her cheeks were flushed with the wind, and her eyes were sparkling with a life and a vibrancy he hadn't seen in them since they'd lost Harry, and, without thinking, he reached out and touched her cheek, only to see her step back and the light in her face instantly disappear.

'It's beginning to get dark,' she said, half turning. 'We ought to start heading back.'

'Oh, I'm sure we can risk a few more minutes,' he said quickly, wanting so much to recapture her laughter, not wanting to return to her cottage where he knew she would shut him out again. 'What made you think of our flat in Killarney?'

'I guess…' She looked out to sea. The breakers were much higher now, the clouds more louring. 'I guess it's because even though it wasn't the greatest flat in the world, it was our home, and I was so happy there.'

'You never objected when I started applying for jobs in England,' he said, pointedly, and she sighed.

'I was so young when we got married, Connor, and my mother said a wife should always follow her husband wherever he wanted to go, and I didn't question that. I know different now. I know it should have been a joint decision.'

'But why did you never tell me you were unhappy?' he demanded. 'Why did you never say, "Connor, this isn't the life I want"?'

'I wasn't unhappy. Unhappy…' She shook her head helplessly. 'Unhappy makes it sound as though I was crying in secret, miserable all the time, and I wasn't. I just felt… detached. As though my life was on hold while I was in London, but eventually I'd start living again.'

He gazed at her uncomprehendingly.

'But, every time I went for a promotion, you were always solidly behind me, saying, "Go for it." Every time I found us a nicer flat, a bigger flat, you seemed so happy, and when I decided to go it alone, to set up my own business, you were thrilled to bits.'

'Because you were,' she admitted. 'I shouldn't have pretended—I see that now—but you were so determined to make it big in England, and money—status—they always mattered much more to you than they did to me. All I ever wanted was enough money for us to get by, a nice place to live in, and…and a family. I would have been more than happy to stay in Killarney, with you working at the local accountant's office, and me in the hospital there.'

'But my career…my own business…' He dragged his fingers through his hair, his eyes bewildered. 'Brianna, I did it all for you, so you wouldn't ever end up like my mother.'

'Your mother?' she echoed in confusion. 'There was nothing wrong with your mother. She was a lovely lady—'

'Who I watched grow old before her time, trying to put enough food on the table to feed myself and my dad, and my three brothers,' Connor said bitterly. 'All her married life she had to scrimp and save, and she never…' He shook his head. 'Brianna, she never got anything pretty, or silly, or frivolous, and I vowed when I watched her, sitting up to all hours of the night, trying to find enough money to pay for the food, and rent, and electricity, that my wife would never have to do that.'

'Connor, it wasn't your father's fault that the only work he could get was occasional because he had emphysema—'

'I know that,' he said impatiently. 'I don't blame him.'

'And your mother *loved* your father,' she insisted. 'Even though they never had much money, there was always laughter in your house, and your mother wanted your father, not the things he could buy her, just as I only ever wanted you and not the fancy flats, or the posh London address.'

'That's easy for you to say when you never had to go without when you were growing up,' he retorted. 'Your parents had their own farm, their own animals, and chickens. They weren't dirt poor like my parents.'

His parents had been poor, she remembered. The tenement flat they'd lived in, in Dublin, had seemed so dark to her when she'd first visited, but it wasn't the darkness she remembered. It was Connor's mother beaming at her, clearly delighted with her son's choice, and his father enveloping her in a hug even though he could barely walk by then.

'I know my parents were more comfortably off than yours,' she said awkwardly, wishing she could somehow make him understand, 'but there was never any shortage of love in your home.'

'You can't live on love, Brianna,' he said, annoyance tingeing his voice, 'not in the real world.'

She opened her mouth, then closed it again.

'Maybe the truth is I'm just a country girl at heart,' she said with an effort, 'and London was just too big, too impersonal for me. Maybe…maybe if we'd had children it would have made a difference. I don't know, I honestly don't.'

For a long moment he said nothing, and when he did speak his voice was low, bleak.

'We both took the decision to turn off Harry's life-support system, Brianna.'

'I know,' she said unevenly. 'I know we did. I'm not… I don't blame you for that.' She took a deep breath. There was something she had to say to him. Something that had revolved round and round in her mind like a canker for the past two years, and, even if his answer broke her, she still had to ask. 'You never really wanted children, did you?'

He swung round to her, his hair streaming back in the wind, appalled horror plain on his face.

'How can you say that?' he exclaimed. 'How can you even *think* it? Harry was my son, my baby, too. We tried for so many years to have him, and when we lost him… How can you say I didn't want him?'

'Then why, when I was pregnant, did you never seemed as excited as I was?' she pressed. 'I couldn't wait for Harry to be born, and yet you… You never went shopping with me for baby clothes, or helped me choose a cot, or—'

'God dammit, Brianna, I was working flat out, twenty-four seven,' he protested. 'I didn't know whether you would want to go back to work after the baby was born so I wanted to make sure we were financially secure. Just because I didn't go shopping with you, or race around our flat doing high fives all the time, doesn't mean I didn't want him.'

And he was holding something back, she knew he was from the way he wasn't quite meeting her eyes.

'Connor—'

'You seem better now than when I last saw you,' he said.

Better. Was she better? She certainly no longer cried herself to sleep every night, no longer woke up in the dark thinking Harry was somewhere in the house, lost, distressed, needing her, but better now…?

'I don't think you ever get over the death of a child,' she said with difficulty. 'You just somehow get through it, one day at a time. At the beginning, after Harry died, there were days when I wondered if I would even make it to the next day, and days when I honestly didn't care if I didn't. I felt so alone, you see, so very much alone, but now… The pain's still there, the ache and the longing for him is still there, but it's…duller.'

'Why do you keep saying you were alone?' he exclaimed. 'You weren't alone. *I* was there, *I* was with you.'

'But I couldn't talk to you, and you…' She pulled her coat closer to her. It was getting colder, so much colder, but he'd asked her a question, and he deserved an answer. 'You didn't seem to…to care the way I did. When we got home from the hospital, you'd taken everything away. His cot, his clothes, his toys—'

'I was trying to make things easier for you,' he protested.

'I thought…if you saw them…it would only make you more upset.'

'And you thought, if they weren't there, I'd *forget*?' she said incredulously, and he flinched.

'I was trying to help, Brianna, to protect you—'

'What you did was take all the decisions away from me,' she declared. 'I might have wanted Harry's room to stay exactly as it was. I might have wanted to burn every single thing in his room, or pack it all away, or give it to charity, but you didn't give me that choice.'

'I'm sorry, but when we lost Harry—'

'Will you stop saying that?' She flared. 'We didn't lose Harry. He wasn't a…a parcel we inadvertently left behind on a train and never got back. He *died*, Connor.'

His face twisted. 'I know.'

'Then why do you never say it?' she demanded. 'Why do you always say we lost him?'

'Lost…died…' A muscle in his jaw clenched. 'What difference does it make? It means the same thing.'

'No, it doesn't. Connor—'

'Has it all gone, Brianna?' he said, holding out his hand to her hesitantly. 'The love we once shared. Has it all gone?'

She stared back at him silently. She didn't want to hurt him. He looked so suddenly vulnerable, so completely unlike the utterly self-confident Connor she had always known, but he had told her he wanted no lies, no half-truths, only honesty.

'I don't know,' she replied. 'I honestly and truly don't know.'

And she turned and walked away from him, leaving him gazing bleakly after her.

CHAPTER FOUR

'HAVE you seen this?' Connor exclaimed, tossing a copy of the *Penhally Gazette* down onto the coffee table in the staffroom.

Brianna glanced dismissively at the front page, and shook her head.

'I don't read the *Gazette*—haven't ever since they printed that disgusting article about Jess. If Vermin has included some snotty comment about the poor quality of my photograph—'

'Read the article.'

Something about Connor's tone had Brianna putting down her mug of coffee, and picking up the newspaper.

'"Abandoned baby found in St Piran Hospital car park",' she read out loud. '"Sister Flannigan of the neonatal intensive care unit…" blah, blah, blah "…baby has been named Harry…"' She frowned up at Connor. 'OK, so it's not the greatest prose style in the world, but I don't see—'

'Read the last paragraph.'

Obediently, she continued reading.

'"The mother has as yet not come forward,"' she murmured, '"but this newspaper can also exclusively reveal that Sister Flannigan is currently…"' Her eyes flew to Connor's then back to the newspaper, '"is currently living with Connor Monahan, an external auditor brought in by the St Piran Hospital board to determine cost-saving measures which could include ward closures."' Slowly she lowered the newspaper. 'How the hell did he find that out, Connor? How, on God's green earth, was Vermin able to find that out?'

'I was going to ask you the same thing.'

'You think I *want* people to know you're my husband?' she said without thinking, then flushed scarlet when she saw the pain in Connor's eyes. 'I didn't mean that—it came out all wrong—'

'I don't give a damn about him knowing I'm staying at your cottage,' he interrupted angrily. 'To be honest, he wouldn't be much of a reporter if he hadn't done some snooping, and he was bound to notice my car sitting outside your home all night. What I want to know is how he discovered why I'm here, in the hospital?'

'Oh, come on, Connor, it's hardly a state secret,' she protested. 'Rumours about why you were coming to St Piran's started filtering out of Admin over a month ago. The only things we didn't know were who you were, and the actual day of your arrival.'

'Brilliant.' He groaned. 'Just brilliant. My assessment is supposed to be hush-hush. *Nobody* was supposed to know anything about it until I'd made my report—the board were quite specific about that.'

'But it's hardly your fault if St Piran's is a hotbed of gossip,' she replied. 'It's a hospital, Connor. Gossip and rumour go with the territory.'

He sighed, and rubbed his fingers wearily over his face. 'I can only hope the board see it that way.'

'You mean, they could fire you?' She gasped, and he grimaced.

'Breach of confidentiality, going public with something

they wanted to keep private… Let's just say they're not going to be very happy with me.'

'But *you* didn't tell anyone,' she protested. 'It was the gossiping staff in Admin. They're the ones who should be torn to shreds, not you.'

'And you'd care if I was?' he said, unable to hide his surprise, and she rolled her eyes in exasperation.

'Of course I'd care,' she replied. 'I know how much your work means to you.'

He'd far rather she knew just how much *she* meant to him. Far rather he could somehow find the right words, instead of always saying the wrong ones. She'd hardly spoken at all this morning over breakfast, and he hadn't dared to. All he'd been able to think, as he'd stared at her lowered head, was how had they come to this, how had they grown so far apart, that they couldn't even make any kind of conversation any more?

'Connor…?'

She was gazing up at him with concern, and he managed to smile. She'd said things hadn't been right between them even before Harry, and maybe she was right. Maybe he'd somehow lost sight of what she wanted in his determination to achieve what he'd believed they both did, but there had to be a way back for them, a way of reaching her.

'What's done is done,' he said. 'All I can do now is try to achieve some damage limitation.'

And not just in this job, he thought as he followed Brianna back to the ward, and the minute she appeared the entire staff fell awkwardly, and all too guiltily, silent.

'I take it you've all seen this morning's edition of the *Penhally Gazette*?' Brianna said, her back ramrod-stiff, but her cheeks, Connor noticed, were pink. 'So, to satisfy your curiosity, I am not conducting an illicit affair with Mr Monahan. He's my husband.'

Megan threw her an 'I'm so sorry about this' look, Chris's mouth fell open, as did the mouths of the other nurses, but Rita was clearly not going to be quite so easily satisfied.

'But I don't understand,' she said, all innocent confusion, as the nurses around her scattered, clearly not wanting to get involved. 'How can Mr Monahan be your husband when you never said you were married, far less to the man who's auditing this hospital?'

'I fail to see why Sister Flannigan needed to tell anyone anything about her private life,' Connor replied before Brianna could reply. 'And she, of course, understands the need for complete confidentiality regarding the nature of my job.'

'Even so,' Rita said, 'I still think—'

'Oh, I wouldn't,' Connor interjected, his voice soft, and velvet, and deadly. 'I really would seriously recommend you don't. But in the meantime,' he added with a smile that would have had Brianna backing off fast, 'why don't you run away and make sure the rest of the hospital staff knows the latest, stop-press new? I'm sure you must be just itching to spread the word, and it will save Sister Flannigan the trouble of having to post a bulletin on the notice board.'

The ward clerk needed no second bidding, and, when she'd gone, Brianna sucked in a shaky breath.

'Remind me never, ever to cross swords with you,' she murmured, 'but thanks. Again.'

'Any time,' he replied, then caught her gaze. 'And I mean that.'

He did, too, she thought. Connor would have thrown himself in front of a runaway horse to protect her, would have gone fearlessly into battle on her behalf at the merest hint of a threat, but sharing his feelings with her... That was something else entirely.

'Yikes, but that was impressive, Connor.' Megan grinned as she joined them. 'But how in the world did Vermin ever find out you were staying at Brianna's cottage?'

'I'm afraid my car's not exactly forgettable,' Connor replied ruefully, 'plus leaving it outside Brianna's house all night... I guess that was just asking for trouble.'

'I suppose so.' Megan sighed. 'But maybe it's better if everyone knows the two of you are married. Some things... it's not always wise to keep them under wraps. When the truth comes out, as it always does, the repercussions can be worse.'

And she was talking about herself, Brianna realised from the dark shadows she could see in Megan's eyes. Not about Connor and her, but about herself, and Connor knew it, too, judging by his slight frown, and she glanced helplessly across at him and, to her relief, he came to her rescue.

'How are all your little patients this morning?' he asked, and Megan grabbed his question with clear relief.

'Our jaundiced baby seems to be making good progress, as is our congenital hypothyroidism little boy,' she replied. 'Amy Renwick's beautifully stable, and all the other babies are doing very well, though I have to say little Harry's a bit too quiet for my peace of mind.'

'How can a baby be too quiet?' Connor asked, clearly puzzled, as Megan walked over to the little boy's incubator and he and Brianna followed her. 'I would have thought quiet meant content, happy?'

'It can,' Megan agreed. 'And he certainly seems to be responding to the surfactant, but...' She shook her head. 'He just seems a bit lethargic, to me.'

'Just because he isn't constantly moving around in his incubator, as some of our babies do, doesn't mean there's anything wrong with him,' Brianna said swiftly. 'As Connor said, he's probably just a very contented baby.'

Megan nodded, but she didn't look convinced, and a chill of foreboding crept up the back of Connor's neck as he stared down at the baby who was lying, unmoving, in his incubator. As Megan had said, there was quiet, and there was quiet, and he had never once heard this baby cry. Brianna might not think there was anything wrong, but he wondered how much of that was denial on her part because the baby did look like their son. Not strikingly so, but enough to make him feel slightly sick inside.

'My gut feeling is we're missing something,' Megan declared, 'so I want those blood results chased up, more X-rays, a spinal tap, a CT-scan—'

'You think he could be brain-damaged?' Connor gasped, and could have bitten off his tongue when he saw Brianna's face whiten.

'I'm not into guessing games, Connor,' Megan replied firmly, 'and I'm probably simply overreacting, and he's actually one contented little boy, but I want to cover all bases.'

'Right,' he murmured, backing up a step. 'OK, I have notes I want to transfer from my phone to my laptop, so I'll…I'll head off to my office and let you get on with it.'

Megan smiled slightly as Connor strode quickly out of the ward.

'He's getting quite attached to our Harry, isn't he?'

'Who wouldn't when this little one is such a cutesy?' Brianna replied, then took a deep breath. 'The spinal tap… Are you thinking sepsis?'

'Hell, Brianna, I'm not thinking anything,' Megan insisted. 'I just…'

'Have a gut feeling.' Brianna nodded.

She'd had them, too, in the past. A nurse's sixth sense

warning that, despite what their monitors and hi-tech machines indicated, there was something not quite right.

'Do you want me to page Babbling?' she asked, and Megan shook her head.

'Let's wait for those blood results, and while we're waiting we'll do a spinal tap before we pull in our resident Cassandra. And speaking of prophets of doom,' she added dryly, 'I think Rita wants a word with you.'

'Oh, joy,' Brianna muttered with feeling, glancing over her shoulder to see the ward clerk clearly attempting to catch her attention, and Megan laughed.

'Just don't kill her, OK?' she said. 'Removing all that splattered blood from the unit…' She grinned. 'Nightmare.'

But it wasn't Rita who wanted to speak to Brianna outside in the corridor. It was Jess, her face alight with excitement.

'I think I might know who the mother of your abandoned baby might be!' she exclaimed without preamble.

Which was good news, Brianna told herself, as she felt her heart give an uncomfortable, and unexpected, dip. It was tremendous news, the very best of news, and yet she found herself having to struggle to return Jess's smile.

'That's…that's brilliant,' she replied, all too conscious that Connor had come out of the nurse unit manager's office, and was listening intently. 'Who is it?'

'Do you remember me telling you some months ago about the girl I saw who gave me a false name?' Jess replied.

'A false name?' Brianna repeated in confusion, and Jess shook her head at her.

'You *must* remember. She came in the day that poor young car mechanic, Colin Maddern, was killed in a car crash. She told me her name was Marcia Johns, and I thought it sounded odd, and it wasn't until she'd gone I realised why. She'd clearly picked the name from one of the pharmaceutical posters on my wall.'

'I can sort of vaguely remember that.' Brianna frowned. 'But what makes you think she could be Harry's mother?'

The counsellor held up three fingers and counted them off.

'Number one, it was very clear to me she'd been deeply in love with this Colin even though she couldn't have been much older than sixteen. Number two, she gave me a false name, and why would she do that unless she was afraid I might make enquiries and find out who she really was and where she lives?'

'Jess—'

'And number three,' the counsellor continued triumphantly, 'even when I spoke to her I felt she was hiding something, that there was something else she wasn't telling me.'

'Did she look pregnant?' Brianna asked, and for a second Jess looked downcast. Then she brightened.

'She wouldn't have if she was only two, or three, months gone, and this must have been…six…seven months ago.'

'Would you be able to give the police a description of this girl?' Connor asked, to Brianna's acute annoyance, and Jess frowned.

'She was blonde—well, more corn-coloured, really—and her eyes were grey, but the trouble is I only saw her twice. Once when she came to the hospital, and once when I was out with Gio in his car.'

'Nevertheless, I think you should tell the police what you know,' Connor declared, and Brianna bit her lip.

What right did he have to interfere, to put in his

pennyworth? The baby's mother's identity had nothing to do with him.

'Jess, you can certainly go to the police if you want,' she said, 'but let's look at the facts here. You don't know the girl's real name, and you don't even know if she was actually pregnant. All you know for certain is she had blonde hair, and grey eyes, and there must be dozens of girls out there who would fit that description.'

'My own granddaughter, Nicola, for a start,' Rita observed as she came out of her office, clearly having been hovering behind her door, listening to every word, 'and I'm telling you this. If the police start stopping every sixteen-year-old girl in the street and asking if she's recently given birth, there'll be hell to pay from the parents.'

Jess flushed.

'Damn, but I hadn't thought of that. I'm so sorry, folks,' she added. 'It just all seemed to fit, but you're right—I don't have enough information, only guesswork.'

'I still think you should speak to the police,' Connor declared, but the counsellor shook her head.

'If I remember anything else, I will, but right now... For all I know I've just put two and two together and come up with five, and that's not going to help anyone.'

'What will happen to Harry if his mother doesn't come forward?' Brianna asked, and Jess sighed.

'When he's well enough, Social Services will arrange for him to go into care or be fostered, until he can be adopted. Look, I know that sounds awful,' she continued quickly, seeing Brianna's expression, 'but there are some really good foster-parents out there.'

'I suppose so,' Brianna said unhappily, 'but it seems a pretty wretched start in life for a little baby.'

'Brianna...'

She could hear the caution in Connor's voice, the concern, but she didn't turn round—couldn't.

'I wouldn't give up hope yet of his mother coming forward,' Jess observed bracingly. 'It's only been two days since you found him, and there could be dozens of reasons for her not coming back to claim him.'

'Yeah, like her thanking her lucky stars she's got rid of him,' Rita declared, and Jess rolled her eyes at Brianna.

'I have to go,' she said. 'I have wall-to-wall clients today—'

'Which reminds me,' Brianna declared. 'When you've a minute, could you have a word with Naomi Renwick? She's been doing marvellously, managing to keep most of her anxieties pretty much under control since her daughter was born, but I get the feeling things are starting to get on top of her, and…'

'You think she needs someone not directly involved with her daughter's medical care to talk to her?' Jess nodded. 'Not a problem. I can't see her today, but I'll definitely drop by tomorrow.'

'Nice woman,' Connor said as Jess hurried away. 'Seems very caring, as well as capable.'

And if he thought that, then maybe Jess's job would be safe, Brianna realised, letting out a silent whoop of joy.

'Her husband's very nice too,' she replied, just in case Connor was eying up the neurology department for cutbacks. 'Gio Corezzi, the neurosurgeon?'

'I'm sure Mr Corezzi is very nice,' Rita chipped in, before Connor could reply, 'but, when you think about it, what do any of us really know about him?'

'What's there to know?' Brianna said in confusion. 'He's a brilliant surgeon, he's Italian, and he's happily married to Jess.'

'He is *now*,' Rita replied, 'but he wasn't nine months

ago, and don't you think it's odd this baby should be found next to his car?'

Brianna turned slowly to face the ward clerk. 'I'd watch what you were saying, if I was you, Rita.'

'I'm only making an observation—'

'No, you're not,' Brianna interrupted, more angry than she'd been in a long time. 'You're saying that Gio—Gio who loves Jess more than he loves his own life—could have had some…some sort of sordid liaison the minute he arrived in St Piran, and then dumped the woman.'

'I'm only pointing out that it's strange—'

'Have you been talking to Kennie Vernon?' Brianna demanded. 'Because if you have, and I hear this repeated anywhere in the hospital, I'm going to tell Gio what you said, and, believe me, the courts take a very dim—and expensive—view of slander. Understood?'

From Rita's scarlet face it seemed she did, and, as she strode into her office, and slammed the door behind her, Connor shook his head.

'What an absolutely appalling woman. Why on earth does the hospital employ her?'

'Because, despite the fact that she's a nosy, interfering gossip,' Brianna replied, 'she is also, unfortunately, very good at her job.'

'Which is a great pity,' he observed, 'because I would have relished the opportunity of recommending she be given her marching orders.'

'At least she only has two more years to work here before she retires.' Brianna sighed. 'Of course, there's every chance I'll probably have killed her before then, but…'

Connor tilted his head at her. 'You've changed, haven't you?'

'In what way?' she asked, puzzled.

'The Brianna I knew would never have chewed Rita's

head off. She might have wanted to, but she would have been far too afraid of hurting someone's feelings.'

'Yeah, well, maybe I don't care so much about other people's feelings now,' she replied. 'Maybe I care more about what is right.'

He smiled, an odd, almost self-mocking smile.

'You don't need me any more, do you?'

Her eyes flew to his. 'Don't need…?'

'When we first got married, I thought—I sort of expected—that I'd always be…' He shrugged a little awkwardly. 'Your protector, I guess. My role was to be Tarzan—'

'And I was Jane?' she said, and try as she might she couldn't stop the corners of her mouth from lifting. 'Um, Connor, I think maybe you should pick a different comparison because somehow I don't ever see you swinging through the trees wearing only a loincloth.'

'You know what I mean,' he said, his cheeks slightly flushed, 'but look at you now. You have your own home—'

'It's rented.'

'A career you've made all by yourself, a circle of friends, and you didn't need my help to get any of those things. In fact, you probably didn't even need me against Vermin.'

'Oh, yes, I did,' she said with feeling. 'Connor—'

'I'm just thinking, you see,' he said, his face suddenly sad, 'if I'm not your protector, your defender, then there really isn't any place in your life for me now, is there?'

He meant it, she realised. For him, there was only one role that a husband should play in a marriage, and because he believed he was now an irrelevance to her, he was giving her the opportunity to say, 'No, you're right, there is no place for you,' and he would leave, and she'd never see him again.

But was that really and truly what she wanted? She'd

thought it was, when he had first come to St Piran's but, now, staring up at him, seeing his face under the fluorescent lighting, she found herself thinking how very tired he looked, how unexpectedly vulnerable, and how his shirt was ever so slightly crumpled. Which was a stupid thing to think, an inconsequential thing, and she knew it was, but she'd never seen him looking anything but perfectly groomed, and she tentatively put out her hand to him.

'Connor, a man needs to be a whole lot more than simply a protector in a marriage, otherwise we women would only ever marry bodyguards or boxers.'

His lips curved into an uneven smile, and he captured her hand in his.

'Then there's still hope for me—for us?'

She wanted to say, yes, she did so want to say, yes, but there were so many unresolved issues between them, and too many questions still unanswered.

'I can't answer that, not yet. I'm sorry,' she added gently, hearing him sigh, 'but you said you wanted me to be honest, and right now, that's all I can say.'

He nodded. 'I guess...' His shoulders lifted, and he forced a laugh. 'I guess it's better than "Goodbye".'

And before she realised what he was going to do, he'd raised her hand and planted a kiss in the centre of her palm. A kiss so gentle that his lips scarcely brushed her skin, and yet she felt a faint flutter of warmth curl and wrap itself around her frozen heart. A faint flutter that deepened and grew when he held her hand close to his own heart and she could feel it beating.

'Bree...?'

He hadn't called her that for such a long time, not for such a very long time, and tentatively she raised her own hand to touch his cheek, saw him close his eyes, and turn his head so his lips almost touched her fingers, and then he let out a muttered oath when the unit door opened and Josh appeared, looking grimly determined.

'No prizes for guessing who he's come to see,' Connor muttered as he released her hand. 'For a bright man, it's sure taking him a long time to get the message that Megan's not interested.'

'Shush,' Brianna whispered warningly. 'What can we do for you, Josh?'

'I didn't realise you guys were married,' he said, and Brianna rolled her eyes.

'Now, that *was* fast, even for Rita,' she observed dryly, and Josh grinned.

'I want to talk to Megan.'

'Josh, do you really think this is wise?' Brianna said uncertainly. 'She clearly doesn't want to talk to you—'

'But I *have* to talk to her,' the A and E consultant insisted. 'Brianna, please, tell her that.'

'OK, I'll tell her, but don't be surprised if she says she's too busy,' she replied, but, as she turned to go back into the ward, she saw Mr Brooke beckoning imperiously to her from outside his office. 'Oh, damn. Look I'm sorry, Josh, Mr Brooke wants me. Connor, could you find Megan, and tell her Josh really needs to speak to her?'

'I'll try,' he replied.

Which was about as much as anyone could do, Brianna thought as she hurried down the corridor towards Mr Brooke.

'This had better be good, Josh,' Megan declared as she came out of the ward, looking both flustered and irritated. 'Unlike you, who seem to have unlimited free time at your disposal, I am really busy.'

'You're always busy, always avoiding me,' he replied, 'but this is important.'

'It always is, according to you,' she said. 'OK, all right. Spit it out, but make it fast. I have a hundred and one things to do.'

'Rebecca's left me.'

For a second there was no expression at all on Megan's face, then, to Josh's dismay, her face whitened with shock.

'Is this because of me?' she said hoarsely. 'Has she heard rumours about me? Josh, I'll speak to her, tell her that what happened between you and I happened years before she married you, and we didn't even have a proper relationship back then, just...' She bit her lip. 'Just one night of madness that should never have happened.'

'Megan—'

'You haven't told her about Stephen, have you?' she exclaimed, horror tingeing her voice. 'You haven't been insensitive enough to tell her that we had a baby, and he died? Oh, Josh, she must be so hurt—so upset—'

'I haven't told her we had a child. I...' He swallowed convulsively. 'Only you and I know that, and only you and I ever will. Look, Megan, I thought... Rebecca leaving me... I thought...I hoped...you'd be pleased.'

'*Pleased?*' she echoed faintly. 'You thought I'd be *pleased* to have been the cause of someone's marriage ending?'

'I shouldn't have said "pleased"—"pleased" was the wrong thing to say,' he declared desperately, 'and you haven't ended my marriage. Rebecca and I... Our marriage has been slowly dying, bit by bit, for years. It was one of the reasons we moved to St Piran, both of us hoping we might be able to salvage it, but I think we always knew it wasn't salvageable.'

'I'm sorry,' she said, sincerity plain in her face. 'Sorry

for Rebecca, sorry for you. Nobody wants a marriage to fail.'

'I think, perhaps, looking back, that I should never have married her,' he replied. 'That it was a mistake.'

She opened her mouth, then closed it again, and backed up a step, her eyes narrowing.

'A mistake,' she repeated slowly. 'It must be really comforting for Rebecca to know she was a mistake.'

'Megan—'

'But, then, I was a mistake, too, wasn't I, Josh?' Megan continued icily. 'You and I making love when we were students—that was another of your mistakes. Oh, and Stephen. I guess he was *a mistake*, too.'

'Megan, listen to me—'

'You *married* Rebecca, Josh, so presumably you felt something for her at one time?'

He had, he remembered, but the feelings he'd felt for his wife had been nothing like the feelings he'd experienced towards the white-faced, angry woman standing in front of him. With Rebecca he'd felt comfortable, at ease, had thought they wanted the same things from life, while with Megan… His feelings had been so terrifying in their intensity that he'd run from them rather than face them. Run because he'd sensed that Megan embodied everything he'd always feared. Commitment, honesty, family, ties.

'I married Rebecca because I thought…' He let out a long, shuddering breath. 'I thought we wanted the same things, but I don't think we ever really understood one another, whereas you and I…'

'You and I *what*, Josh?' Megan said her voice tight.

'I'm sorry, I'm not explaining this very well—'

'You think you can just take up where you left off, don't you?' she interrupted, disbelief plain in her voice. 'You think that because your wife has walked out on you, I'll be only too ready and willing to leap back into your bed again despite what you did, despite…' Her voice broke slightly. 'Despite you taking everything of any value from me.'

'No, of course I didn't think that,' he protested.

'Then why is it so all-fired important to you that I should know?' she demanded. 'Why do you think it would matter a damn to me whether your wife has left you, or if you're still happily married to her?'

He took a step towards her, and saw her back away still further.

'Look, I'm saying this all wrong,' he faltered. 'It's coming out all wrong.'

'Oh, I think it's coming out just right, Josh,' she retorted. 'Thanks for the update on your private life, but there was no need for you to hurry up here to tell me. I could have waited like everyone else until Rita spread the word.'

And she walked away from him, leaving him gazing in despair after her.

'You want *me* to be the new nurse unit manager?' Brianna gasped as Mr Brooke beamed benignly at her. 'But… why?'

'Because you're not only my most qualified member of staff, you're also the best,' he replied as she gazed at him, open-mouthed. 'And—believe me—those two things don't always necessarily go together.'

'But…'

'I know it's going to mean getting to grips with a whole lot of unfamiliar paperwork, but the job's yours, if you want it. You do want it, don't you?' he added as Brianna stared at him uncertainly.

Nurse Unit Manager. It was her dream job, the job she'd always wanted. Of course she knew it wouldn't be easy. The post carried a huge amount of responsibility, and she'd seen how many hours Diego Ramirez had needed to put in just to keep on top of all the paperwork, but she wanted it, she really did, except... If she accepted the post it would mean there was no possibility of her going back to Connor. He was a city man, with a high-powered city job. He'd never move to Cornwall in a million years, which meant, if she accepted the job, she would be accepting that her marriage was over.

Well, it is, isn't it? her mind whispered, and she took an unsteady breath.

'Mr Brooke, I'm flattered—immensely flattered—you think I can do this—' she began, and Richard Brooke put up his hands quickly.

'I can hear a "but" coming and I don't want to hear a "but". Look, I've put my neck on the line here by telling Admin I want it to be an in-house appointment, so will you at least think about it? I can't give you too long to make up your mind, because we desperately need a replacement for Nurse Ramirez, but—frankly—I can't see why you're hesitating.'

Neither could Brianna as she walked slowly out of Mr Brooke's office. It was what she'd always wanted, to be in charge of the nursing staff in a unit, and if the consultant had only asked her last week she wouldn't have hesitated for an instant, but now... Now she didn't know what to do, and the last person she could talk to it about was Connor.

At least she was able to avoid his far-too-acute gaze for the rest of the day. When she got back to the ward, Megan told her he'd gone to Men's Surgical to interview the staff there and, for a moment, Brianna considered confiding in the paediatric specialist registrar, but one look at Megan was enough to tell her that her friend was struggling with her own private demons. Whatever Josh had so desperately wanted to talk to Megan about, it had obviously upset her greatly, but her closed face did not invite conversation and, for once, Brianna was relieved when her shift was finally over.

'He's still going to be here tomorrow, you know,' one of the night nurses said with a chuckle when Brianna made her customary stop at Harry's incubator to check on him before she left.

'I know,' Brianna replied, 'but I just like to say good-night to him. He doesn't have a mother so...' She shrugged awkwardly. 'Silly of me, I guess.'

The night nurse said nothing, but Brianna knew what the woman was thinking. That she was breaking the cardinal nursing rule of 'Never get too close, never become too involved, with a patient' but she wasn't getting too close. She was simply doing her job, doing the best she could for little Harry, and if a small voice in the back of her head was whispering its own warning, that small voice was just overreacting.

Exactly as Connor was, she thought ruefully when she eventually got home, and found him pacing up and down in front of her cottage.

'I was beginning to think your car had broken down,' he said. 'That I was going to have to come out and rescue you before the storm breaks.'

Actually, he was right about the storm, Brianna realised as she squinted up at the sky. Ominous black clouds were rolling in from the west, the wind was picking up, and small drops of rain were already beginning to fall.

'I thought you might be tired when you got back,' he continued, hovering behind her as she trudged wearily into her cottage, 'so I tossed a coin, and put some chilli in your microwave when I heard your car.' He glanced anxiously at her. 'I hope that's OK?'

'Sounds good,' she said with an effort. 'Have I time to

shower and change? I always think I smell so overpower-
ingly of disinfectant when I get back from the hospital.'

'Sure.' He nodded. 'You've plenty of time. In fact, take
all the time you need. I've already set the table, and put on
the fire, so there's nothing for you to do.'

She wished there was as she went upstairs, and show-
ered, and changed into a pair of jeans and a sweater. She
wished even more that he would stop being so helpful, so
thoughtful, when she didn't want him to be any of those
things. It just made everything so much harder.

'You seem a bit preoccupied tonight,' he observed after
they'd eaten a largely silent meal. 'Nothing wrong at the
hospital, I hope?'

'Everything seemed pretty quiet when I left,' she murmured. 'Megan's going to chase up little Harry's blood tests
results. They generally take seventy-two hours, so they're
not late, but I know she'll be a lot happier when she sees
they're normal.'

And if they're not?

The unspoken words hung between them, and neither
of them voiced them.

'What did Mr Brooke want to see you about?' Connor
asked as he began to collect their dirty dishes.

'Oh, nothing important,' she said evasively. 'Just boring
stuff like paperwork.' He didn't believe her, she knew he
didn't, and quickly she went over to the sink, and turned on
the tap. 'I'd better get these dishes done. It's getting wilder
out there, and we might get a power cut.'

And it was getting wilder, she thought as she stared out
of her kitchen window into the darkness. The wind was
now buffeting the house, and squally rain was battering
against the windows. She loved it when it was like this, so
wild and tempestuous. It always made her feel like a small

bird in its nest, listening to the elements raging around her, but Connor clearly didn't share her feelings.

'Not very seasonal weather, is it?' he observed with a grimace as he picked up a tea towel. 'March… You think of daffodils, and crocuses, and spring approaching, not howling gales and rain.'

'You can get wild weather at any time of year,' she replied, and he nodded.

'It rained a little on our wedding day, didn't it? Your mother said June would be a lovely month to get married in, and it rained.'

'Rained?' she exclaimed. 'Connor, it poured solidly all day, and we had hailstones, and a gale-force wind.'

'Oh, come on,' he argued. 'There might have been the odd shower or two—'

'I don't know whose wedding you're remembering, but it certainly isn't ours.' She chuckled as she added some washing-up liquid to the water in the sink. 'The train at the back of my dress got completely soaked when my father and I had to make a mad dash from the car to the church, we had to have all the wedding photographs taken in the reception hall instead of outside the church because nobody could stand upright, and Ellie Warburton, my flower girl, fell in a puddle, and cried for the duration of the reception.'

'Lord, so she did.' He grinned. 'Why was Ellie one of your flower girls anyway? She didn't seem to know you from a bar of soap.'

'She didn't, but my mother insisted because she's some sort of cousin of mine, twenty zillion times removed, and her family would have been deeply offended if she hadn't been asked.'

'Right,' he said, clearly none the wiser as he began

drying their plates. 'OK, so the weather was bad, but everything else was perfect.'

'You corrected Father Driscoll during the ceremony.'

'I did not!'

'You did too,' she declared. 'When he said, "Do you, Connor, take Brianna Kathleen to be your lawfully wedded wife?" you said, "I, Connor, take Brianna Kathleen O'Donnell to be my lawfully wedded wife." You're not supposed to say the bride's surname.'

'I didn't want there to be any mistake,' he protested. 'I thought there might be dozens of Brianna Kathleens in the world and I wanted to make sure I was marrying the right one—my one.'

'My mother was mortified.' Brianna smiled as she remembered. 'She said she'd never be able to look Father Driscoll in the face again when he told her afterwards that he'd never been corrected in church before.'

'Well, like I said,' Connor declared defensively, 'I wanted to be sure I was marrying my Brianna Kathleen.'

'And then my Uncle Joe sang his party piece at the reception,' Brianna continued with a shudder. 'My father promised faithfully not to let him, but halfway through the evening he said, "Sure, Brianna, a wedding's not a wedding unless Joe sings *Delilah*."'

'Does your Uncle Joe ever remember the right words?' Connor asked, and Brianna shook her head.

'Never.' She laughed.

Laughed with such genuine amusement and happiness that he put down the tea towel and caught her soapy hands in his.

'Do you know what I remember most about our wedding day?' he said softly. 'It was turning round when I heard the wedding march and seeing you coming down the aisle towards me. You looked... Oh, you looked so beautiful it took my breath away, and I thought, Connor, lad, how in the world did you ever get so lucky to win this angel?'

'Flatterer,' she said shakily, trying to pull her hands free without success.

'Gospel truth,' he said huskily. 'All I could think was, Please let her reach my side quickly, before the gods or the fairies snatch her away and keep her all to themselves.'

'Connor, I'm getting soap suds all over the floor,' she protested, completely unnerved by the intensity of his gaze, but he ignored her.

Instead, he reached behind her, and, before she could stop him, he'd unplaited her hair and spread it out over her shoulders.

'Your hair was loose,' he murmured, 'just like it is now, and you had flowers threaded through it. Flowers that matched your bouquet, all the colours of the rainbow they were, but paler, and the scent…'

'Freesias…' she whispered, feeling her heart rate pick up. 'They were freesias.'

'And when I said I would honour and keep you, in sickness and in health, until death us do part, I meant every single word.'

She had meant those words, too, but it hadn't been his death, or hers, that had parted them, it had been Harry's.

'Connor…'

'You never told me you were going,' he said, sliding his hands down her back. She could feel his hands trembling— or perhaps she was. She couldn't be sure. 'How could you do that, Brianna? How could you just disappear, never telling me where you were, whether you were safe?'

'I was wrong,' she said unevenly. 'I see that now, but all I could think was if…if I could just get away from you, from London, from everything that reminded me of Harry, I'd be all right.'

'But why Cornwall—why here?'

'Because…' She closed her eyes, and took a shuddering breath. 'Nobody would know me. Nobody would be able to point their finger and say, "She's the one whose baby died. She's the mother whose baby died," and because they couldn't I thought—not that I would forget—I won't ever forget—that it might be…easier.'

'Bree, I have missed you so much,' he whispered, his voice constricted. 'Missed seeing you, missed hearing your voice, and I have so missed holding you.'

He was holding her now. He'd wrapped his arms around her, and then, gently, oh, so tenderly, he kissed her, and when she sighed against his mouth she heard him groan. A groan that seemed to come from deep down inside him, and it felt so good to be held, so good to be kissed, that she kissed him back, and felt him shudder, but as his kiss became more insistent, and he pulled her even closer to him, she suddenly felt the patent evidence of his arousal, and she flinched. She didn't intend to, didn't mean to, but she flinched, and she knew he felt it because she could see the pain of rejection in his eyes as he drew back from her.

'Connor, I'm sorry,' she said unevenly, 'so sorry, I don't know why I—'

'I understand,' he interrupted bleakly.

How could he, she wondered, when she didn't understand her reaction herself? That she'd wanted to be held by him, she'd wanted his arms around her, but, the moment she'd realised that just holding her wasn't enough for him, something inside her had frozen, something within her had screamed, No.

'It isn't you,' she said. 'It's me.'

'It's all right, *a chuisle mo chroí*,' he said with an effort. 'You've had a long day and you're tired. You should get some sleep. I'll finish clearing up in here,' he continued when she tried to interrupt. 'You get yourself away to your bed.'

'But—'

'Goodnight, Bree.'

He had turned back to the sink, and slowly she walked away from him but, when she reached the kitchen door, she half turned.

A chuisle mo chroí.

Pulse of my heart.

It was what he'd called her on their wedding night, when they'd made love for the very first time, and she wanted to say something, knew she should say something, but no words would come. No words that would explain what she couldn't explain, and, as a tear trickled down her cheek, she slipped away, leaving him gazing out of her kitchen window, his face in shadow.

CHAPTER FIVE

Rita was smiling. It was never a good sign when Rita smiled. Either the ward clerk had discovered a new and particularly juicy piece of gossip, or she was about to dump someone in a very large pile of manure, and, whichever it was, Brianna knew she wasn't up for it today—she really wasn't.

'Something I can help you with, Rita?' she said with an effort as the ward clerk sidled up to her, her face distinctly conspiratorial.

'It's about your husband, Sister Flannigan…'

Don't go there, Rita, Brianna thought. If you value your life, don't ask me why I've been living alone in Cornwall for the last two years while I have a husband in London, because, if you do, you're dog meat.

'What about my husband?' she said coolly.

'Just that it's such very good news that he *is* your husband.' Rita beamed. 'I mean, I think we can now safely say my job is completely secure because he'd never shut down any department you worked in.'

Incredible, Brianna thought as she stared at the ward clerk. The woman was completely incredible, but she wasn't about to let her get away with it.

'I don't think we can say that at all,' she replied. 'In

fact, I can assure you my husband would never allow any personal bias to influence him.'

Rita tapped the side of her nose, and winked.

'Of course you *would* have to say that, wouldn't you, Sister, but enough said, message understood, and I won't say another word.'

Which will be a first, Brianna thought grimly, but as Rita bustled away, her anger swiftly faded.

She had such a headache this morning, such a blinding, thumping headache. She'd scarcely slept last night, had spent every hour tossing and turning, reliving what had happened in her kitchen. At least Connor hadn't appeared in the unit yet, and she wondered if his absence was deliberate. She wouldn't have blamed him. She'd allowed him to kiss her, allowed him to hold her, and then she'd rejected him. Rejected him for no reason she could fathom except, perhaps, her body had been telling her that she no longer wanted him, that there was nothing left of their marriage.

'You OK?'

She half turned to see her staff nurse, Chris, regarding her with concern, and grimaced slightly.

'I have a thudding headache this morning,' she replied. 'And before you ask,' she added, 'I've taken something for it, so I can't take anything else.'

It had been Connor who had pressed the aspirin into her hand, she remembered. He'd taken one look at her face this morning, made her breakfast, pressed the pills into her hand, then suggested she should consider taking the day off, but his solicitude had only made her feel worse.

'I'm afraid I'm going to add to your headache,' Chris declared. 'Vermin's here.'

Brianna swore under her breath.

'If that low-life thinks he can get another interview with me—'

'Actually, he wants to speak to Mr Brooke, though why he thinks our consultant will be able to give him any more information than you did is anyone's guess.'

'Where is he—Vermin, I mean?' Brianna asked.

'I've left him cooling his heels in the corridor.'

'The hospital sewer would have been better,' Brianna replied, then frowned slightly. 'You did tell him Mr Brooke has a clinic later on this morning, after his ward rounds, so he's not going to be able to see him any time soon?'

A look of mock dismay appeared on the staff nurse's face.

'Oops, but would you believe I completely forgot to tell him that?'

'Not for one second.' Brianna laughed. 'But it will do Vermin no harm to kick his heels for a couple of hours.'

'That's what I thought,' Chris declared smugly, then her eyes lit up. 'Your husband's here.'

'Is he?' Brianna said dully, without turning round, and Chris dug her gently in the ribs.

'Talk about dark horses. I don't know how you managed to keep quiet about him. He's quite something, isn't he?'

'You said he was scary,' Brianna reminded her, and the staff nurse's smile widened.

'I still think he is, but in a *very* sexy sort of a way.'

Chris thought her husband was sexy. So, too, she remembered, had the wives and girlfriends she'd sat next to at the dinner parties Connor had taken her to in London. Dinner parties whose sole purpose seemed to be for the businessmen there to boast about the deals they'd struck. Networking, Connor had called it, as she'd sat in silence throughout these meals, feeling completely out of place and uncomfortable. Nobody had ever been interested in her when they'd discovered she was a nurse. Zero networking opportunities, the men had clearly thought, while their wives and girlfriends had eyed Connor up, and tried to flirt with him.

'Couldn't you at least *try* to make conversation?' Connor had said impatiently after one of the dinners. 'The other wives, and girlfriends… They always seem to be able to find something to say, but you just sit there like a little frightened mouse.'

And she'd wanted to say that most of the wives and girlfriends' conversations seemed to involve flirting with him, but she hadn't.

'Your head's still sore, isn't it?' Connor declared as he walked across to her and Chris bustled away.

'It's better now,' she lied, and saw his left eyebrow lift.

'Yeah, right. How's everyone doing?' he continued, glancing at the incubators around them. 'How's the baby who was abandoned?'

'His name is Harry, Connor,' she said irritably. 'He seems quite content.'

Quiet, you mean, Connor thought, and quiet doesn't mean the same as content, you know it doesn't, but you won't accept that.

'Brianna—'

'The little girl with jaundice is progressing well,' she said.

She was deliberately changing the subject, he knew she was, but he knew better now than to push.

'Should the soles of her feet, and the palms of her hands, be quite so yellow?' he asked, and saw Brianna smile.

'They're that colour because she had pretty severe jaundice. Every newborn has elevated bilirubin—it's a by-product of haemoglobin, which is usually eliminated from the body as waste—and it's that excess bilirubin which makes so many babies' skin look yellow. Normally, the baby's liver will start functioning at full speed within a few days, but sometimes they need a little help, which is what we're giving her.'

'And the baby who has congenital hypo…hyper…'

'Congenital hypothyroidism,' she finished for him. 'It occurs when a baby's thyroid gland is absent or under-developed at birth.'

'That sounds serious.'

'It used to be. In the past, a baby could end up with permanent mental retardation, and development delay, but we can now give a synthetic thyroid orally.'

'Fascinating,' he said, meaning it, and she laughed.

'There have been an amazing number of medical ad-vances in recent years, and what is even more marvellous is scientists keep on discovering more and more treatments, more and more cures. Although…' The light in her eyes suddenly dimmed. 'Not for everything.'

He knew what she was thinking, and he didn't want her to be thinking of their son, and this time it was he who changed the subject.

'Little Amy. Mrs Renton's daughter—'

'Mrs Renwick,' Brianna corrected him. 'She's progress-ing well, too. Naomi isn't doing quite so well but I'm hoping Jess will be able to help her.'

'Maybe we should have seen someone like Jess,' he murmured. 'After Harry…you know…'

'Died,' she prompted. 'Just say it, Connor. Nothing awful is going to happen if you say that word.'

But he didn't.

'Maybe we shouldn't have thought we could go it alone, cope alone,' he continued, his face bleak. 'Maybe if we had accepted the help the hospital offered, things might have been…easier.'

'Maybe,' she murmured, and she looked so suddenly lost that he longed to reach for her, to put his arms around her, but he'd tried that last night and she clearly hadn't wanted his touch.

Was it too late for them? he wondered as he saw her smile past him, and he turned to see Mrs Renwick had arrived. He didn't want to believe it was, but he never seemed able to say the right thing, never seemed able to do the right thing, to give her what she wanted, needed, but that didn't mean he wasn't going to try. It wasn't in him to give in without a fight, and this fight involved the highest stakes he'd ever played for. This was one he simply couldn't lose.

'I'll leave you to it,' he said in a low undertone as Mrs Renwick walked towards them. 'I have notes to copy over to my laptop, and I think Amy's mother looks as though she needs you.'

Naomi did, Brianna thought. There were dark shadows under her eyes, and her face was white, and pinched.

'I think you should go home to bed, Naomi,' she said as Connor slipped away. 'Forgo your visit today.'

'I'm fine,' Mrs Renwick replied. 'I just had a very bad migraine yesterday, the third this week, and they tend to wipe me out.'

Stress, Brianna thought. Mega-, mega-stress.

'Your daughter had an excellent night, and is currently moving all over the place inside her incubator,' Brianna declared with a smile. 'Every time I put her to the top, she manages to make her way to the bottom. In fact, I reckon you've got a future long-distance walker there.'

Naomi didn't even attempt to raise a smile.

'You're very kind, Sister, and I know I must seem like the most negative person in the world to you—'

'Of course you're not.'

'But sometimes it's so hard to keep on being positive. My daughter is the most wonderful, precious, joy to me, but…' Naomi bit her lip. 'I told my husband last night she's going to be our only child. I can't go through this again—I just can't.'

'And statistically you won't have to if you decide to give Amy a little brother or sister,' Brianna said gently. 'Though having had one premature baby does put you at a twenty to forty per cent risk of having another one, look at it another way. It also means there's a sixty to eighty per cent chance you won't.'

Naomi nodded, but Brianna could tell she hadn't convinced her, and she wasn't surprised. Having a premature baby was so emotionally draining for parents. All too often, every day seemed to bring with it a new challenge, a new worry, but if anyone could reassure Naomi it would be Jess.

And the counsellor was as good as her word. She arrived midafternoon, and bore Mrs Renwick off to the parents' room, smoothing over Amy's mother's protestations of not having time by insisting she needed a cup of coffee but hated drinking it alone.

'She's good, isn't she?' Megan observed when Jess and Mrs Renwick had gone. 'I wish we had the time to do what Jess does, but we're so constantly snowed under with all the medical procedures we need to perform on the babies that the emotional needs of the parents far too often get overlooked.'

'She's one of a kind, that's for sure,' Brianna agreed. 'And…' She looked over her shoulder to make sure there was no one near, least of all Rita. 'I *think* her job is safe.

Connor hasn't said so—not in so many words—but he *did* say she was very capable so…'

'It's looking good.' Megan breathed with a sigh of relief. 'He didn't…' She grimaced. 'Look, I know I shouldn't be asking you this, but he hasn't given you any indication of which department he might be recommending for the chop, has he?'

'I'm afraid Connor doesn't talk about his work,' Brianna said ruefully. 'Actually, Connor's not big on talking, full stop.'

'One of the strong, silent types, eh?' Megan smiled, but Brianna didn't.

'You could say that,' she murmured, then cleared her throat. 'I've not seen Josh today.'

'Hopefully he's finally remembered which department he's actually supposed to work in,' Megan replied tersely.

Which pretty well ended that conversation, Brianna thought, but she couldn't leave it there even though she knew she probably should. The specialist paediatric registrar looked as ragged as she felt.

'Megan, I know this is none of my business—'

'His wife's left him, Brianna.'

'Josh's wife?' Brianna said faintly. 'But…'

'Yes, I know,' Megan said, her lips twisting slightly. 'Rita must be really beginning to lose her touch if she hasn't managed to pick up that juicy bombshell yet.'

The specialist registrar's voice was hard, brittle, but if ever a woman was close to tears Megan was.

'I think I saw his wife once at a hospital reception,' Brianna said carefully, 'but I've never met her.'

'She was—is—very beautiful,' Megan said. 'But not happy. I don't…' She took a shallow breath. 'I don't think she was very happy.'

'Was…?' Oh, lord, but this was so very hard to say, but

Brianna knew she had to say it. 'Was that what Josh wanted to talk to you about yesterday?'

Megan nodded.

'Not that it's of the least interest, or consequence to me, of course,' she said. 'I mean, whether he's married or single. It's not like he and I…' Her voice trembled slightly. 'It's not like we mean anything to one another.'

'Oh, Megan—'

'Don't,' the specialist paediatric registrar said quickly. 'Please, don't give me any sympathy, or I'm going to embarrass myself, and you.'

'You could never embarrass me,' Brianna said softly. 'Not ever. Josh's wife leaving him… Do you think…are you hoping…?'

'I don't know what I'm thinking, or hoping,' Megan replied with difficulty. 'I just wish…oh, how I wish…he'd never come to St Piran's, that I'd never had to meet him again.'

Because now I have to think about things I don't want to think about, remember things that might have been better kept buried. That was what Megan was saying, and Brianna understood exactly how she felt.

'Megan, listen to me—'

The specialist paediatric registrar shook her head warningly, and Brianna glanced over her shoulder to see Connor approaching.

'Great timing, Connor.' She sighed as Megan hurried away, and her husband's eyebrows rose.

'I can always go away again,' he offered, and she shook her head.

'Too late, I'm afraid.'

And for more than one thing, she thought with dismay when she saw Mr Brooke sweeping into the ward, all smiles. If Vermin had convinced the consultant that she would be willing to give him another interview she was going to throw a hissy fit. A big one.

'Ah, Sister Flannigan,' Mr Brooke declared. 'The very person I was hoping to see.'

'Mr Brooke, if this is about Vermin—I mean Kennie Vernon,' she began, 'he's had all he's ever going to get out of me.'

'Who's Kennie Vernon?' the consultant said with a frown.

'The reporter who wanted to talk to you. The man who's been hanging about in the corridor for the last couple of hours?' she added helpfully. 'Looks like a very bad eighties rock star, dressed all in black, goatee beard?'

'I haven't seen anyone like that this morning,' Mr Brooke replied in confusion. 'No, this is about you, my dear, and my offer,' he continued, ushering her away from Connor to the side of the ward. 'I really need your decision soon. Time and tide, remember, Sister Flannigan, time and tide.'

'Yes. Absolutely,' she muttered, wishing—oh, wishing so much—that the consultant would simply shut up.

He had such a very carrying voice even when he was trying to talk in an undertone, and though Connor was apparently deep in conversation with Chris he'd always been able to listen to two conversations at once.

'As I told you, I can't wait long,' Mr Brooke continued. 'You know how short-staffed we are, and, if you decide to step up to the plate and accept the nurse unit manager's job, we'll need to advertise for a replacement for your job.'

'I appreciate that,' Brianna said. *Please shut up*, she thought. *Please just shut the hell up.* 'And I'll give you my decision by the beginning of next week.'

'Good. Good.' Mr Brooke beamed, then turned on his heel. 'Ah, Connor. A word with you, if I may? I've had a talk with ENT, and they say you can interview their staff next week if that suits you.'

Brianna didn't wait to hear her husband's reply. She was too busy heading for the ward door. She was due a break, and she intended taking it right now. Not in the canteen—with her luck, she'd probably run into Josh—but the nurses' staffroom sounded good. A coffee, and more aspirin for her head sounded even better.

But her hoped-for peace and quiet didn't last long. Within minutes, Connor had appeared and seemed hell-bent on tearing the staffroom apart.

'Can I assume you've lost something?' she said as he turned his attention to the waste paper bin after riffling through the magazines on the coffee table.

'A memory card.' He frowned. 'I've been transferring my notes on the various departments I've been assessing from my phone to my laptop via a memory card, and I can't find it.'

'That'll teach you to be so damned hi-tech.' She could not help but chuckle. 'Use a clipboard and pen next time like the rest of us ordinary mortals.'

'Oh, very funny,' he said irritably, and she took pity on him.

'What does this memory card look like?'

'About the size of a small matchbox, but wafer thin.'

Brianna stared at the abandoned magazines, the un-washed coffee cups and discarded biscuit packets that littered the nurses' staffroom, and shook her head.

'Yeah, well, good luck with finding something that small in this place.'

'Maybe I left it at your cottage,' he murmured. 'I've already searched the nurse unit manager's office, and it's definitely not in there.'

'Don't you have a back-up memory card?'

He nodded. 'I do, but I'd still like to find the original. It has a lot of sensitive data on it.'

'Should MI5 be worried?' She grinned. 'Maybe we should—'

The rest of what she'd been about to say died in her throat when the staffroom door opened, and Jess appeared, her face shining.

'You look as though you've just won the lottery,' Brianna declared, and Jess's smile widened even further.

'It's something much, *much* better,' the counsellor said excitedly. 'I've remembered something else about the girl who I think could be Harry's mother. It came to me when I was talking to Mrs Renwick.'

'When you were talking to Naomi?' Brianna said, and Jess nodded.

'Naomi was wearing an initial necklace, and I suddenly remembered that the girl I met was wearing one, too. In fact, the second she saw me looking at it, she pushed it down into her blouse.'

'Can you remember what the initial was?' Connor asked when Brianna said nothing.

'M—no, N— Or was it M?' Jess shook her head with frustration. 'It was one or the other, I'm positive.'

'So what you're saying is we should be looking for a teenager, with blonde hair, and grey eyes, who may—or may not—have been pregnant when you saw her, and whose first name could start with the initial N or M?' Brianna declared. 'Jess, apart from the fact that this girl could be a complete red herring, think of all the girls' names that start with those initials. It would be like looking for a needle in a haystack.'

'Not that big a haystack,' Connor observed thoughtfully. 'Knowing it's either N or M would cut out a lot of teenagers in the area.'

'And what use is that?' Brianna said irritably. 'Even if we made a list of all the girls in the area whose Christian names begin with the letter N or M, we can hardly phone them up and say, "Have you been pregnant recently?"'

'Flora,' Jess declared. 'Flora Loveday's the health visitor for Penhally. I could phone her—ask if she's noticed any girl who fits my description. A girl who might suddenly have become rather plump recently.'

'And Flora will give you a complete roasting if you ask her that, you know she will,' Brianna protested. 'She'll cite patient confidentiality, and she'd be right.'

Jess grimaced.

'I know.' She sighed. 'It's just… Oh, this is so frustrating. I feel I'm so close, so very close to finding this girl. All I need is one extra piece of the jigsaw.'

'Jess—'

'I wonder if I could get a list of all the families in the area?' the counsellor continued. 'The electoral roll only gives the names of those old enough to vote—but…'

'And what then?' Brianna said, trying and failing to hide her irritation. 'I don't want to rain on your parade, but maybe you should just give up on this amateur sleuthing, and leave it to the police to track down Harry's mother. Personally, I think she's most likely to be someone from outside the county, rather than a local girl.'

'No, she's local,' Jess declared emphatically, 'and I still think it's the girl I met.'

'Oh, for heaven's sake, why can't you just accept it's not?' Brianna said tartly, and Jess blinked.

'Brianna…' Connor cautioned, and she rounded on him.

'It's true, Connor! This whole scenario of the girl who Jess happened to meet, who may, or may not, have given her a false name, and who may, or may not, be Harry's mother, is crazy, you know it is. I understand that Jess wants to help, but enough is enough!'

'Right,' Jess murmured, beginning to back away, her cheeks darkening. 'I'm sorry—you know—for bothering you like this, and I won't do it again.'

And before either Connor or Brianna could say anything she'd left the staffroom, and Connor shook his head at Brianna.

'That wasn't very kind.'

'Maybe I don't feel kind,' Brianna retorted. 'Maybe I've just heard enough of Jess's half-baked theories to last me a lifetime.'

'And maybe you don't want this baby's mother to come forward at all,' he said, and Brianna got to her feet impatiently.

'Of course I do. I just think—'

She never did complete what she'd been about to say. The emergency alarm sounded, and she was out of the staffroom in a second.

'What's wrong—what's happened?' Connor asked, hurrying after her.

'It's one of the babies,' Brianna replied, frantically washing her hands. 'Something's badly wrong with one of the babies!'

And it was Harry. Harry's monitors which were sounding the alarm, and Megan and Mr Brooke were already at his incubator.

'Pulmonary haemorrhage, Brianna,' Megan murmured, as she hurried round the incubator to insert another IV line. 'Looks like patent ductus arteriosus.'

'What does that mean?' Connor asked, trying not to get in the way, and wishing the monitors would stop making their shrill noise.

'Left heart failure,' Brianna replied tightly, and

Connor closed his eyes, feeling as though someone had punched him.

Heart failure. Their son had died because of an inherited heart defect, which meant it wasn't the same, but it felt like it.

'Why didn't that show up before?' he demanded. 'He's had enough X-rays and scans. Shouldn't it have shown up then?'

'It can sometimes happen to babies who have respiratory distress syndrome,' Megan explained. 'We don't know why, but when it happens it happens fast.'

'I want an echocardiogram, and I want it now,' Mr Brooke ordered.

Chris was gone in a flash, and somewhere in the ward Connor could hear one of the babies crying as though it somehow knew that…

Don't go there, his mind warned. *Don't even think that.*

'Is there anything I can do?' he asked as he saw Brianna flipping switches, changing lines, completely in control, though both her face and lips were white.

'Just keep out of the way,' she replied. 'Are we looking at thoracoscopic surgery?' she continued, glancing across at Mr Brooke.

'There's a strong risk of laryngeal nerve damage if I do that,' he declared as Chris appeared with the echocardiography machine. 'Plus I could end up with a ligation of the pulmonary artery if I make even the tiniest mistake.'

'There's also the mortality rate to consider,' Megan pointed out.

'Which is currently one per cent,' Brianna replied, as she applied some gel to Harry's chest. 'Pretty good odds, I'd say, plus you don't make mistakes, Mr Brooke.'

The consultant shook his head.

'Nice compliment, Sister, but all surgeons can make mistakes, and, with a baby as little as this, we could be also looking at damage to the thoracic duct.'

'Yes, but thoracoscospic surgery is much less risky than a thoracotomy,' Brianna argued, 'and we're running out of time here.'

'Agreed.' He nodded as Chris placed the transducer on Harry's chest. 'OK, let's see what we've got.'

To Connor, the echocardiogram seemed to take an eternity. The pictures on the screen meant nothing to him, but they clearly meant something to Brianna, Megan, Chris and Mr Brooke, because there was a lot of muttering and a lot of pointing.

'What have you decided?' he asked when Chris removed the transducer, and both Megan and Brianna looked at Mr Brooke.

The portly consultant chewed his lip, then nodded.

'Thoracoscospic surgery. Dr Phillips, Sister Flannigan, you'll assist.'

Chris was already pushing Harry's incubator out of the ward, and as Brianna made to follow her Connor put out his hand to stay her.

'He is going to be all right, isn't he?' he said.

'I don't know,' she replied, her bottom lip trembling slightly. 'I honestly don't know. Mr Brooke's a brilliant surgeon. He has lousy people skills, but when it comes to operating, he's the best, but... Look, why don't you go back to my cottage?' she continued. 'I don't know how long the op will take—'

'I'm going nowhere,' he said, but as Brianna turned to leave he added, 'Would it be wrong of me to wish you all luck? I know on the stage it's considered very bad luck to say that, so they say break a leg, but—'

'We'll take your good wishes,' Brianna declared. 'With this one we're going to need all the luck we can get.'

And she was gone, and Connor stood in the centre of the ward, knowing he had never felt quite so alone, while the other nurses bustled about, a kind of normality returned for them.

It had been so different with their own son, he thought as he walked slowly out of the ward and down to the nurses' staffroom. He and Brianna had sat together in the consultant's room, holding one another's hands in a vice-like grip as though that might somehow keep Harry with them, while the consultant had explained very gently, and very kindly, that there was nothing he could do. The damage to Harry's heart was too severe, he'd said, and the kindest thing would be to switch off his life-support system.

The kindest thing.

Connor gritted his teeth. He'd wanted to hit the consultant when he'd said that. Kind shouldn't have meant simply allowing their child to die. Kind should have meant the medical staff doing everything they could, never giving up, not them recommending they switch off the only thing that was keeping their son alive.

With an effort, he pushed open the door of the staffroom and went in. Were there any more depressing places than empty staffrooms and waiting rooms? he wondered as he sat down and let his head fall back against the seat. Brianna had been right when she'd said being able to do something was infinitely preferable to having nothing to do but wait, but wait he would, for as long as it took.

Wearily, Brianna walked down the corridor towards the staffroom. Chris had told her Connor was there, had been there ever since they'd taken Harry to Theatre, and she was grateful, so very grateful, that he'd stayed.

Gently, she opened the door in case he'd fallen asleep, but his head snapped round immediately, and she could see the hesitation in his eyes, the desire to know, and yet the fear of knowing, too.

'He's fine,' she said. 'The op was textbook perfect, and he's back in his incubator, breathing well.'

She saw him exhale, then his eyes scanned her face.

'How are you?'

'Shattered,' she admitted. 'Relieved. Happy.'

'Then, let's go home, Bree,' he said, getting to his feet. 'You're just about out on your feet, and you said yourself he's out of the woods, so let's go home.'

To his surprise, she didn't even attempt to argue, which proved how exhausted she was, and she didn't protest either when he put some food into the microwave when they got home, then pulled out a chair for her.

'I know you probably feel too tired to eat,' he said when the lasagne was ready, 'but you really should try.'

And obediently she picked up a fork. And she did eat, though he very much doubted if she knew what she was eating, but at least she ate.

'You're not still worrying about him, are you?' he said when she finally pushed her plate away, and she shook her head.

'When I was in Theatre,' she murmured, 'all I could think was how fleeting life can be. How, in the blink of an eye, everything can suddenly change, and you never get to do the things you want, or say the things you should, and then it's too late.' She raised her eyes to his. 'Do you remember asking me whether I was sorry I had left, or sorry you'd found me?'

He gazed back at her, clearly confused, obviously wondering why she was saying this now, and then he nodded.

'I remember.'

Say it, Brianna, she told herself. *Tell him everything because you might not ever have this moment again.*

'I was sorry you'd found me because I didn't want you to find me.'

His face twisted. 'I see.'

'No, you don't, because I haven't finished yet,' she said swiftly. 'I left you because I knew I had to get away from everything. From our flat, my memories and, yes, from you because every time I looked at you I saw Harry. Harry dying in my arms, Harry's life slipping away from him, and you…' She took a breath. 'You were slipping away from me, too, and I didn't want to face the fact that not only had my son died, but my marriage was over, so it was better to hide, better not to have to face that truth.'

'But our marriage wasn't over,' he declared, bewilderment plain in his blue eyes. 'Why in the world did you think it was?'

'Connor, even before Harry was born, we might have shared the same flat, but we barely talked, hardly ever saw one another—'

'I was *working*,' he protested. 'You know what working in the city is like. If you rest on your laurels, you don't get considered for the big deals, and I had to keep on working hard if I wanted to stay in the game.'

'But even when you came home, you used to shut yourself away in your study,' she said, 'and I'd wait, and wait, and maybe, if I got lucky, you'd share a few words with me, and I'd go to bed and fall asleep alone, not knowing what you were thinking, or…' Her eyes skittered away from his. 'If you still loved me, or you'd found someone else.'

'You thought I was *cheating* on you?' he exclaimed, plainly dumbfounded. 'Bree, I have *always* loved you, and I always will.'

'Then why did you increasingly shut me out?' she cried.

'And don't tell me you didn't, because you did, you know you did. You hardly ever held me, or kissed me, and…' A faint tinge of colour crept over her cheeks, but she was going to say this come what may. 'We only ever made love if I asked you to.'

He bit his lip savagely, and, at first, she didn't think he was going to answer her, and then he met her gaze, and she saw pain and heartache in his eyes.

'I know we did, and I am sorry, so sorry, but…' He shook his head blindly. 'Oh, hell, but this is so hard for me to say because I don't want to hurt you. You've been hurt so much already.'

'Say it, Connor,' she urged. 'Whatever it is, just say it.'

'I knew…' He took an uneven breath. 'I knew how much you wanted a child—I wanted a son or a daughter, too—but as the years went by, and you didn't become pregnant, I felt…' His eyes tightened. 'You didn't want to make love to me any more—not to me. That all I'd become for you was a sperm donor. Someone you needed to go through the motions with to get yourself pregnant, not someone you wanted to be there for you, not someone you wanted to give you pleasure.'

'You thought that?' she said, horror-stricken by his revelation. 'Oh, Connor, why didn't you tell me, why didn't you say something?'

He clenched his jaw. 'It's hardly the sort of thing you can say to your wife, is it?'

'But it would have explained so much,' she declared. 'I thought you didn't want me any more, that you'd fallen out of love with me, and I was so scared to ask you outright because I thought, If he's found somebody else, I won't be able to bear it.'

'There's never been anyone but you, Bree,' he said simply. 'There never will be.'

'I'm so sorry,' she said with a sob. 'Sorry I made you feel…redundant. I never meant to. I just… I wanted a baby so badly, but my desire for one shouldn't have made you feel you meant less to me than achieving that. Can you ever forgive me?'

To her surprise, he half turned from her, his face pain-racked.

'Don't, Bree, please, don't apologise to me. It only makes me feel worse.'

'Worse?' she echoed. 'What do you have to feel so badly about? I was the one at fault, not you.'

'You've no idea how I wish to God that was true, but it isn't, it isn't,' he said, his voice ragged.

'Connor—'

'You asked me before whether I wanted Harry, and the truth is…' He lowered his head for a second, and, when he looked up again, his eyes were agonised. 'Bree, when you were pregnant, you were so ill all the time. I used to listen to the other men at work, the ones whose wives were pregnant, saying how well their wives looked, how happy and blooming, and every night…' He balled his hands into fists. 'Every night I would go home and find you with your head down the toilet, being sick again. Nothing you ate seemed to stay down, and instead of looking blooming you just seemed to get thinner and thinner.'

'It was a difficult pregnancy,' she said, gently putting her hand on his arm. 'Some just are, and I didn't care about being sick. I just wanted our son.'

'I know you did, but…' He drew in an anguished breath. 'I hated him before he was born, Bree. I knew it was wrong,' he said quickly when she drew back from him, appalled. 'I knew I shouldn't feel that way, but seeing you so ill, knowing he was the one doing it to you… I was frightened. So frightened I was going to lose you, and no baby was worth losing you for, so, yes, you were right, I didn't want him.'

'Not even when he was born?' she said, her eyes dark, her voice barely audible. 'Didn't you want him even then?'

'When he was born…' Pain twisted across his face. 'Oh, Bree, when I saw him I suddenly knew why you hadn't given a damn about being so sick all the time. He was so beautiful, wasn't he, and I thought…' His voice shook. 'I thought, This is my son. This beautiful, tiny, little person is *my son*. And I thought my heart was going to burst with joy, and then…all hell broke loose. The doctors and nurses were running everywhere, and they took him out of your arms, and there were all these tubes and wires, and I thought, Stop it, stop what you're doing, you're hurting him, and you mustn't hurt him.'

'I remember,' she said, her voice suspended.

'And when the doctors said he wouldn't live…' Connor shook his head, and something like a sob broke from him. 'All I could think was, It's my fault. God has listened to me, and decided, OK, if you don't want him, I'll take him away from you.'

'No, Connor, oh, no!' she exclaimed, instinctively reaching for him, but he lurched to his feet, evading her. 'It wasn't like that, you mustn't think like that. No words, or thoughts, of yours could have caused Harry's heart condition. It was an inherited heart defect. A horribly, cruel, inherited defect.'

'I still blame myself,' he said raggedly, screwing his eyes shut. 'Every time I go to bed at night, and close my eyes, I still see him, so small, so fragile, and looking so much like you.'

'I always thought he looked like you,' she said unsteadily, and Connor shook his head.

'You, he was all you, and when he died... Bree, half of me died with him because I'd failed him, I'd failed you.'

'You didn't—you didn't,' she cried, getting to her feet and clasping his hands tightly in hers. 'Connor—'

'All my life I've set myself goals, Bree,' he said hoarsely, 'and I've ticked them off one by one, but the one thing I knew you wanted above everything else was a child, and when they said we should turn off his life support...' A shudder ran through him. 'I wanted to fight with them, to tell them to go to hell, to tell them *I* would save our son if they couldn't, but I couldn't save him, I knew I couldn't, and to feel I had no control, no power to alter anything... that broke me, Bree.'

She stared at him blindly, so wanting to help him, to somehow find the right words to say to help him, because she had never seen him like this before, a man in torment.

'Why didn't you tell me any of this?' she exclaimed. 'Oh, Connor, you should have told me this.'

'You were going through hell, and I...' He bit his lip. 'I didn't want to burden you with how I felt.'

'But we could have shared it,' she protested. 'All I could see was that you didn't seem to care—not like I cared. You wouldn't talk about him—'

'Because I always seemed to say the wrong thing,' he said. 'If I didn't talk about Harry you got so angry, and if I did talk about him you cried, and I couldn't...I couldn't bear to see you cry when there was nothing I could do to make it any better.'

'All I ever needed was for you to let me cry, Connor,' she said, her voice breaking. 'Just for you to let me cry and for you to…to talk about Harry, so I could feel you understood, that you felt the same way I did.'

'I did, Bree. Oh, God, how I did,' he said. 'I wanted him back, too. I wanted to be able to hold him again, and keep him safe, but I couldn't keep him safe, and…' A tear trickled down his cheek, and he pulled his hands out of hers. 'I'm sorry… I have to… I have to…'

He was walking swiftly towards the staircase and she ran after him.

'Connor, wait,' she begged, trying to catch hold of his arm, but he shrugged her off, and began climbing the stairs.

'Leave me be, Bree,' he said over his shoulder, his voice choked. 'I don't…I don't want you to see me like this.'

'Like what?' she cried. 'Showing me you care, showing you feel? Connor, it's not shameful to cry, it's not a sign of weakness.'

He came to a halt at the top of the stairs, his face averted.

'It is,' he said, his voice cracked. 'I should be supporting you, not the other way round.'

'Can't…can't we support one another?' she exclaimed. 'Comfort one another?'

'Bree, enough, please,' he entreated, and she walked round him, and caught his face in her hands.

'Don't, Connor, oh, please…don't shut me out,' she said, 'not this time.'

He screwed his eyes tight shut again, but it didn't help. She could see tears trickling down his cheeks, running into his nose and mouth, and for a moment he stood rigidly still and then suddenly he reached for her, and she caught him and, when he buried his face in her neck, he broke down completely.

Broke down and cried in great shuddering, gasping sobs

that tore at her heart, making her cry, too, but she didn't try to stop his tears, knew how much she'd hated it when he'd tried to stop hers, and knew, too, how much he needed to finally cry.

'I'm sorry, so sorry,' he said eventually, his voice raw, his eyes red-rimmed. 'You shouldn't have had to witness that.'

'Yes, I should,' she insisted, cupping his face with her hand. 'You loved Harry, just as I did.'

'Would…?' She saw him swallow hard. 'Would you stay with me tonight, Bree? I just want to hold you,' he added quickly. 'Nothing else—I just want to hold you, and not… not be alone any more.'

And she nodded, and took him to her bed, and held him close, and eventually they fell asleep, wrapped in one another's arms. And some time in the middle of the night, he woke her, and reached for her, and she knew what he wanted, and this time she wanted it, too. This time she wanted to make love to him, and, as she touched him, and he touched her, they both cried again. Not the racking, heart-rending tears they'd shed in the past, but tears that were healing tears, tears for a past they could not change, that left them clinging to one another, neither of them ever wanting to let go.

CHAPTER SIX

CONNOR smiled slightly as he rolled over onto his back, and heard the small, protesting sigh that Brianna made as she followed him and nestled up again against his side.

It was going to be all right. Everything was finally going to be all right. When he and Brianna had made love last night it had been both a wonderful and also a cathartic experience for them both, and this morning he felt new, reborn, as though the world was yet again full of endless possibilities, instead of the dark and empty place it had been for the last two years.

Today is the first day of the rest of your life.

Who had said that? He couldn't remember, but today was most definitely the start of a new life for both of them and he wasn't going to screw it up this time round. This time he would get it right.

Gently, he put his arm round her, not wanting to wake her, but, when he rested his chin on the top of her head, he heard her yawn.

'What time is it?' she murmured.

He squinted at the bedside clock. 'A little after seven.'

'I have to get up,' she said regretfully. 'Auditors might be able to lie in bed for as long as they like, but nurses don't have that luxury.'

He tightened his grip on her, not wanting to let her go,

and knowing he wanted her all over again as she stretched against him.

'Pity about that,' he said, tracing the length of her spine with his finger and feeling her shiver. 'I was kind of hoping…'

'I'm sure you were,' she said, as she raised her head and looked up at him, her brown eyes dancing, before rolling over onto her back, 'but I need a shower, and some breakfast.'

He propped himself up on his elbow and gazed down at her.

'We could shower together. Very eco, that. Saving water, heating, and think how much faster we'd get clean if we washed each other.'

'Yeah, right.' She chuckled. 'And like I don't know that the state of the planet would be the very last thing on your mind if we got into the shower together. Connor, I don't have time.'

'But I can be real fast when it comes to showering,' he insisted. 'See, what I'd do first would be to put some soap on my hands, and then I'd do this…'

Slowly he smoothed his hands over her shoulders, tracing the length of her collarbone.

'Connor, I really don't—'

'And then,' he interrupted, his voice becoming a little huskier as his palms slid down onto her breasts. 'I'd wash you here. Very carefully, of course,' he continued, hearing her suck in her breath sharply as he began sliding his hands up and down and over each breast, circling and circling them until the nipples peaked, 'because I know how very sensitive your breasts are.'

'Connor, I…I think you should stop now,' she said faintly, and he shook his head at her.

'You see, that's the beauty of us showering together.

You wouldn't have to think,' he murmured. 'And after I'd washed your breasts—because I'm a really thorough sort of a man—I'd cover you with plenty of soap down here,' he continued, sliding his palm down her stomach, slowly, oh, so very slowly, until he cupped her. 'And then,' he added, as he began to stroke and stroke her, easing her thighs further and further apart, 'I'd do this, though of course you'll just have to try to imagine the soap. How very wet it would be, how very warm, how…liquid.'

'I'm…I'm trying not to.' She gasped, biting her lip when his finger slipped inside her and he continued to stroke her, and she felt the heat beginning to build. 'Connor…please… *please stop*!'

'Hey, but it sure does take a lot of effort to get you really clean, doesn't it?' He chuckled as he increased the pressure of his fingers, and she began to writhe beneath him. 'Maybe I'd also need to do this…'

And he bent down and replaced his fingers with his tongue. Gently at first, licking into her so gently, and then his tongue began to probe further, and further inside her, and she put her hands on his head, and arched up against him, as she felt the throbbing begin, the pulsing begin.

'Connor, oh…oh, my…oh, my *God*!'

And suddenly she jerked and convulsed, shaking and trembling, her heartbeat drumming in her ears as the heat went everywhere.

'Good?' he whispered in her ear, and she nodded breathlessly.

'Very good, amazingly good, stupendously good.'

'And there was you thinking it would take me for ever to get you clean if we shared a shower,' he said with a wicked grin.

She stared back at him for a heartbeat, then, before

he knew what she was doing, she had pinned him onto his back.

'My turn now,' she said, her eyes gleaming. 'My turn to play torturer.'

'Really?' he said huskily, exhaling sharply when she began tracing her fingers down his chest.

'Oh, absolutely.' She nodded as she bent her head, and licked one of his nipples, and then the other, and heard him gasp. 'It's only fair, after all. In fact…' she continued, as she slid her hand down his stomach, and he tensed with anticipation. 'In fact…'

'In fact, what?' he whispered as she suddenly sat up.

'Sorry,' she said, her eyes dancing with devilment. 'I'm afraid this is going to have to be put on hold, because I've just noticed the time, and if I don't hurry up and have a proper shower I'm going to be late.'

'*Brianna!*'

'Yes?' she said, her lips curving, as she slipped out of bed and headed for the door.

'I take back what I said about you being an angel,' he protested. 'You're a witch!'

'Probably.' She grinned.

And he laughed. Witch or angel, he honestly didn't care. She was his again, and that was all that mattered.

Except it wasn't, he realised when he grabbed a quick shower after she'd had hers, and hurried down to the kitchen. Normally, the percolator would be on, and the table would be laid, but this morning none of those things had been done. She was standing by the kitchen window instead, gazing out, and, when she heard him come in, the smile that greeted him was tentative in the extreme. Something had clearly happened between the shower and the kitchen, and that something was making her think, and he didn't want her to think, to have any doubts.

'Fruit juice and cereal for breakfast as usual?' he said brightly.

'Fine,' she replied, retrieving two bowls from the cupboard and putting them on the table.

'Coffee or tea? It will have to be instant if you want coffee,' he added. 'It will take too long if we wait for the percolator.'

'Instant coffee,' she murmured. 'And plenty of it. I find I need lots of caffeine in the morning nowadays.'

'Me, too, or I'm hell to live with.' He grinned. 'Or hellier than I would be.' He frowned. 'Is there such a word as hellier?'

'I expect so,' she said. 'Or if there isn't, there should be.'

Something was most definitely wrong, he thought as he switched on the kettle, then took some orange juice out of the fridge and filled two glasses. Everything had been perfect, just perfect, and now she looked nervous, unsure, as though there was something she wanted to say but wasn't quite sure how to phrase it.

The job, he suddenly realised. It would be that damn job Brooke had offered her. He'd overheard the consultant asking her about it, and she clearly wanted to take it, but she'd realised he wouldn't want to move here, and she was right. Penhally and St Piran were probably very nice for holidaymakers who weren't big on excitement, but what sort of work would he get here? Hell, he'd be reduced to making spreadsheets, and advising the local butcher and baker on their tax returns. Well, it wasn't a problem. There must be dozens of nurse unit managers' jobs in London, and he'd help her scour the nursing magazines for them, and then she could have what she wanted, and he could, too.

'Something wrong?' he said, deliberately giving her an opening, but she shook her head.

'No, no problem,' she replied with a smile he didn't buy for a second.

OK, he thought. Give her time, give her space, don't crowd her, she'll mention the job when she's ready.

'Cream or milk on your cereal?' he asked. 'Actually, scrub the cream,' he added with a frown as he noticed the use-by date. 'You know, you really will have to go shopping.'

'I'll do it before I come home tonight,' she murmured, then he saw her take a deep breath.

Here it comes, he thought. Here comes the 'Mr Brooke has offered me the job I've always wanted, and I don't know what to do about it', so say the right thing this time, Connor, or you're toast.

'I was just thinking about Harry,' she said, taking him completely by surprise. 'The baby I found, not our son,' she added quickly, 'and I was wondering…if his mother doesn't ever come forward…how would you feel…?' She rearranged the salt and pepper cruet on the kitchen table. 'How would you feel about us adopting him?'

Oh, *hell*. He'd known she was getting far too close to this child, much too involved, but he'd never imagined anything like this, hadn't for one second seen this coming.

'Bree—'

'If his mother never claims him,' she said quickly, 'he'll be sent to a foster-home, and though I'm sure they're wonderful places—nothing like the orphanages of the past—they're not like a real home, are they? Connor, we could give him a home, be his parents,' she continued, eagerness plain in her eyes. 'I know he wouldn't be ours in the sense of us being his real mother and father, but we could give him so much.'

'I understand that,' he began carefully, 'but, sweetheart, we're both still young, and though I know it took us a long time to conceive Harry, that doesn't mean we couldn't try for a child of our own again.'

'*No!*' she said vehemently. 'The heart defect Harry was born with, it's an inherited condition, so it could happen again, and to wait for nine months, feeling him—or her—growing inside me—always wondering, always fearing, never knowing… I can't do that, I *can't.*'

'But—'

'The little Harry in the hospital…he *needs* me, Connor, and we have so much love we could give him.'

Slowly he walked over to her, and put his hands on her shoulders, forcing her to look up at him.

'I know we do, but, Brianna, are you sure you want this child for the right reasons?'

She shook her head impatiently.

'What better reasons could there be than me wanting to give him a home, parents, love?'

'You could do that for our own child—'

'I've explained to you why I won't risk that,' she declared. 'Weren't you listening—didn't you hear what I said?'

He *had* heard, he thought. Much more than she probably wanted him to hear.

'Bree, what you're saying is, you want a baby, but you want a no-risk baby,' he said gently. 'You want the baby in the hospital because, though he has health problems, they're health problems that can be cured, and you'll be able to take him home. You're scared, Bree,' he continued as she tried to interrupt. 'You're scared of the unknown, of what might happen if we try for another child—and I can understand that, I feel the same way—but that isn't the right reason to adopt this child.'

'I want him because I can give him what he doesn't

have,' she protested, shrugging herself free from his hands. 'A mother, a father, a home. Why is that so very wrong?'

'It isn't, if it was the whole truth, but it isn't, you know it isn't. Bree, after Harry died, I read up on heart defects. They can be detected now by antenatal screening at eighteen weeks—'

'And then what?' she interrupted. 'If the scan discovered there was something wrong, do you honestly think I would opt for an abortion? I'd have to carry on with the pregnancy, knowing...' She took a ragged breath. 'Knowing that the baby inside me was going to die, just like Harry died, and I don't think I'd be able to survive that.'

He wanted to argue with her. He wanted to tell her that perhaps it wouldn't happen, that maybe the odds would fall on their side this time, but she looked so stricken, and the Harry in the hospital did need a home. Would it be so very wrong to agree to what she wanted even though he knew, instinctively, that it was for all the wrong reasons?

'Connor?'

She was waiting anxiously for his reply, and he sighed.

'Even if I agree to this, it's only been four days since you found him. His mother could still come forward.'

'A normal mother wouldn't have left her child for four hours, far less four days,' she argued back. 'And much as I don't want to agree with Rita, maybe she's right, maybe Harry's mother doesn't want him, which gives us all the more reason to give him a home, where he'd be wanted.'

'And then there's the actual adoption process,' he continued. 'There are couples who have been on waiting lists for years, and just because he's in your ward doesn't mean you can jump the queue.'

'I know that—I understand that,' she insisted, 'but we could try. Will you at least agree that we could try?'

Her eyes were large, pleading, and he wished he could

think of something to say that would dissuade her. He didn't want her to be hurt again, he so desperately didn't want her to be hurt, but he knew how high the odds were against any adoption agency fast-tracking them to the top of their list, and those odds were too high.

'Connor. Please,' she continued softly, and he sighed, then nodded reluctantly.

'If the baby's mother doesn't come forward, we'll see if adopting him is possible,' he said, and saw her face light up with a smile that tore at his heart.

'Thank you,' she said fervently. 'You won't regret it, I know you won't.'

He hoped to heaven he wouldn't, as he watched her hurry across the kitchen to take the cereal packet out of the cupboard, her step light, her lips still curved into a happy smile. He could only hope to heaven that everything would turn out all right.

'You're looking very happy this morning, Sister,' Naomi Renwick declared.

'I feel happy.' Brianna smiled. 'It's a lovely spring morning, all of the babies had an excellent night, including your daughter, so what more could I wish for?'

'My wish would be to take my daughter home,' Naomi replied. 'I know, I know,' she continued as Brianna opened her mouth to interrupt, 'she's doing really well, and in a couple of weeks you're going to try feeding her orally, but…'

'You want to take her home now,' Brianna finished for her, and when Mrs Renwick nodded, she put her arm round her. 'It *will* happen, honestly it will. Good grief, even Mr Brooke is happy with her, and you won't often hear me putting the words "Mr Brooke" and "happy" in the same sentence.'

Naomi chuckled. 'That's what Mrs Corezzi said yesterday. She's very nice, isn't she?'

'She's one of the best.'

'And so are you, Sister Flannigan,' Mrs Renwick declared, and, before Brianna realised what she was about to do, Naomi had leant forward and kissed her cheek. 'In fact, if there was an award for nurse of the year, you'd get my vote.'

'And now you've got Sister Flannigan completely speechless.' Megan laughed as she joined them. 'And that takes some doing, I'm telling you.'

Naomi laughed, and Brianna laughed, too, but her cheeks were burning when she accompanied Megan across the ward.

'That was very nice of her to say,' she murmured. 'Not that I am—or could be—nurse of the year, but—'

'Brianna, you're damn good at your job so no more of this false modesty,' Megan insisted. 'And talking about jobs,' she continued, lowering her voice, 'a little bird in the shape of our portly consultant tells me you're going to be our new nurse unit manager?'

'I haven't accepted the job yet, Megan,' Brianna replied quickly. 'I'd like to, but it's…complicated.'

'One of the complications wouldn't happen to be a certain man who has a very definite spring in his step this morning, would it?' Megan said, her eyes twinkling, and Brianna smiled.

'Connor, and I… We had a long talk last night—'

'I'd say you did a lot more than talk, judging by how you both look today,' Megan said shrewdly, and, when Brianna crimsoned, she chuckled. 'Knew it. So, what's the problem?'

'I do love him, Megan,' Brianna replied. 'I loved him when I married him, and the love's still there. A bit bruised, a little bit battered, perhaps, but it's still there, and this time I think we could make our marriage work, make it a partnership of equals, but...'

'Not here in St Piran.'

It was a statement, not a question, and Brianna bit her lip.

'What would he do here, Megan? His whole career is centred around London. Coming to hospitals like St Piran's... It's a one-off commission, not a permanent job.'

'He could change his life, his career,' the paediatric specialist registrar pointed out. 'People downsize all the time, throw up their high-powered jobs and move to the country to keep chickens or pigs.'

Brianna let out a giggle. 'Can you honestly see Connor keeping chickens or pigs?'

'Well, no,' Megan conceded, 'but I'm sure there's lots of other things he could do if he put his mind to it.'

'How can I ask him to do that?' Brianna protested. 'He's happy where he is.'

'So, in this partnership of equals,' Megan said slowly, 'you're going to be the one who has to give up everything, and return to London?'

Return to London. Just the thought made Brianna's heart plummet. Return to their modern flat, the anonymous streets, to feeling as though her life was on hold again.

Except it wouldn't be like that, she thought as her eyes drifted past Megan to little Harry's incubator. If everything went well, she would have Harry, she would have a child, and that would make everything different. It would.

'It will work this time,' she said firmly. 'I'll make it work.'

'If you say so,' Megan replied. 'Just...'

'Just what?' Brianna asked, seeing her friend's face grow suddenly serious.

'Don't tell Mr Brooke you don't want the job, at least not yet. Connor will be here for another four or five weeks, so take that time to make sure you've both resolved everything between you.'

'I will.' Brianna smiled. 'But you worry too much.'

'Probably,' Megan admitted, 'but just be careful, OK?'

There was nothing to be careful about, Brianna thought as she walked over to little Harry's incubator, and smiled down at him. Everything was going to be fine. She just knew it, could feel it. Harry had come through the operation with flying colours, and already she could see he was brighter, more alert, and Connor had just been trying to protect her when he'd talked about the difficulties of adoption. The authorities were bound to see they were an ideal couple. They were both still young, were comfortably off, had been married for ten years, and she'd give up work, be a stay-at-home mum, so Harry would never have to come home from school to an empty house. And there were so many parks in London, it would almost be like being in the country. And her parents would love him, she knew they would, and—

'Brianna.'

'Are you trying to give me a seizure?' she protested, whirling round to see Connor standing behind her. 'Please don't creep up on me like that, not when I'm miles away.'

'I saw that.'

Something was wrong, she realised. His face was carefully blank, his eyes even more so, and, when she smiled encouragingly up at him, he didn't smile back.

'Hey, whatever it is can't be that bad,' she declared, and saw him flinch.

'There's someone outside you need to see,' he said.

Even his voice sounded strange, as though it was being forced out of him.

'Look, if it's Vermin again,' she began, 'you can tell him—'

'It's not Vermin. It's…' He shook his head. 'I think you should come.'

'Connor, you know I don't like surprises,' she protested. 'Can't you just tell me who it is?'

He didn't answer. He simply walked over to the ward door and opened it, and she sighed.

'This is crazy,' she grumbled. 'I'm really busy right now, so I'm warning you, whoever it is had better want me for a very good reason.'

He still didn't say anything and, when she first went out into the corridor, she was none the wiser. Rita was standing there with a face like stone. No big surprise there, she thought wryly. Jess was beaming broadly at her, but, then, Jess always had a sunny expression, and to Jess's left stood a large, jolly-looking woman in her early forties whom Brianna didn't recognise at all.

Blankly, Brianna glanced back at Connor. Was this a deputation of some sort, a fundraising committee? Puzzled, she shifted her gaze back to the three women, and then she saw her. Standing awkwardly behind the jolly-looking woman, looking, oh, so shy and nervous, was a young girl. A young girl who couldn't have been any more than sixteen. A young girl with corn-coloured hair and large grey eyes, and Brianna dug her fingernails into the palms of her hands until they hurt.

'My name's Marina Hallet,' the jolly-looking lady declared, 'and this is my daughter, Nicola. She's the one who left the baby in the car park. She's Colin's mother.'

'Colin?' Brianna repeated, through lips grown suddenly dry.

'That's his name,' the teenager said softly. 'What I called him—after his father.'

'And we know one another, don't we, *Marcia*?' Jess smiled, and Nicola Hallet looked shamefaced.

'I'm sorry about lying to you that day in the hospital, Miss Carmichael—'

'Her name is Mrs Corezzi now, Nicola,' Rita declared irritably. 'Can't you at least try to get something right for once in your life?'

Nicola looked crushed, and Jess leant towards the girl, a gentle smile on her face.

'Nicola, please call me Jess. All my friends do,' she added, and Brianna heard Rita give a very deliberate sniff.

A sniff that everyone completely ignored.

'I should have told you my real name,' the teenager continued awkwardly. 'I should have said my name was Nicola Hallet, but…'

So Jess had been right, Brianna thought dully. The initial necklace that the girl she'd seen wearing *had* been either an N or an M. It was an N.

'Look, why don't we all go into the staffroom?' Jess suggested. 'It will be a lot more comfortable than standing out here in the corridor.'

'I'd really like to see my grandson,' Mrs Hallet said quickly, and Brianna saw Rita wince.

'And you will,' Jess declared, 'but I'm sure Sister Flannigan must have lots of questions for you.'

'Yes, of course,' Brianna said automatically.

But she didn't want to ask any questions, she didn't want to know anything at all about the teenager, or her family.

She just wanted them to go away, and give her back her dream.

'Aren't you coming in with us?' she said as the four women trooped into the staffroom, and Connor didn't move at all.

'I can't,' he said softly, 'you know I can't. Patient confidentiality, remember?'

He was right, she knew he was, but she suddenly felt so very alone, and he must have sensed it because he clasped her hands tightly.

'I'll be right out here,' he said. 'I won't go anywhere. I'll stay right out here, and wait for you in the corridor.'

Which was where she wanted to be, she thought as she stiffened her back and walked into the staffroom in time to hear Mrs Hallet tell Jess her family owned a fruit-growing farm near Penhally.

What difference did it make what kind of farm the Hallets owned? It wasn't important, it didn't matter, and before she could stop herself she rounded on Nicola.

'Why did you leave your son—abandon him?' she demanded.

Her words were harsh, she knew they were as she saw the teenager flush and heard Jess suck in her breath, but she didn't care. She wanted answers. Little Harry deserved them.

'The silly girl was frightened to tell us she was expecting a baby,' Mrs Hallet declared before her daughter could answer. 'We didn't even know she was going out with Colin Maddern from the garage, far less that she was pregnant. If only she'd told us. When I think of all those months when she must have been so frightened…' Mrs Hallet shook her head. 'I don't know how she coped, I really don't.'

'And you didn't realise—didn't notice your own daughter was pregnant?' Brianna exclaimed, not pretending to hide her disbelief even though Jess was staring at her with clear dismay.

'I know I should have done,' Mrs Hallet admitted, 'but what with the work on the farm, and my family of seven… You see, there's always something happening, some crisis, and Nicola… She's always been the quiet one, the one with her head stuck in a book, and…' She smiled apologetically at her daughter. 'She's always been a little on the plump side so I didn't notice any change in her.'

'I wore lots of baggy clothes,' Nicola murmured, 'and like Mum said, there's always so much going on in our house no one noticed I was getting bigger.'

And she looked so young, so very young, Brianna thought, feeling a hard lump in her throat that no amount of swallowing seemed to move. 'How old are you, Nicola?' she asked.

'Sixteen. Sixteen years and four months to be exact,' the girl added hurriedly.

As though those four months made any damn difference, Brianna thought. Nicola was still a mother, while she… She was never going to be one.

'Why did you leave him in the car park?' she exclaimed. 'Nicola, he could have *died* there!'

The teenager's eyes filled with tears.

'I was bringing him to the hospital because I knew there was something wrong with him,' she replied. 'When I tried to feed him he didn't seem to know what to do, and his breathing wasn't right, but the first person I saw was Grandma, and I knew she'd have a go at Mum, say it was all her fault that I'd got pregnant at fifteen. But it wasn't Mum's fault. Colin and I… We never intended to make love—we were going to wait—but…'

'These things just happen,' Jess said, shooting Brianna

a puzzled glance, and Nicola nodded and wiped her nose with the back of her hand.

'Colin…he said we'd get married if I found out I was pregnant, and I know we would have, because he loved me, and I loved him, but then…' The tears in the teenager's eyes began to spill over. 'He was killed, and he never knew… He never knew he had a son.'

And I think I knew him, Brianna thought dully as Jess leant forward and pressed a handkerchief into the teenager's hand, and she remembered the day she'd had trouble with her car months ago, and she'd stopped at the garage in St Piran, and the young mechanic there had mended it for her.

'Your Colin… He had black hair, and a lovely smile, didn't he?' she said, trying to keep her voice even but knowing she was failing miserably.

'You knew him?' Nicola said eagerly.

'I met him once,' Brianna replied. 'And I remember his smile.'

And how I'd thought that my Harry might have looked just like the young mechanic, if he'd lived and grown up.

'Why didn't you come back later, after your grandmother had gone?' Jess asked, and Nicola bit her lip.

'I meant to—I intended to,' she said, 'but Colin's breathing seemed to be getting worse, and then I saw you. I remembered how kind you were before, and I know I should have told you I was pregnant, but I was scared you'd tell Grandma, and she'd make me get an abortion, and I didn't want to have an abortion.'

'No one would have made you have an abortion,' Nicola's mother declared, shooting Rita a look that defied her to argue. 'You loved this boy, and he loved you, and your father and I would have helped.'

'But why didn't you just give the baby to Jess?' Brianna

protested. 'Why leave it where it might not be found for hours?'

'I guess I panicked,' Nicola replied. 'I recognised the car—I'd seen Mrs Corezzi—Jess—out in it, and I thought it was hers, that she was leaving the hospital so she'd be sure to find my son. I waited,' she added quickly. 'I didn't just go. I waited until you picked him up, so I knew he was safe.'

'And the first we knew of any of this was when she broke down in tears over that photograph in the paper,' Mrs Hallet said. 'That was when the whole story came out.'

'Can I see him?' Nicola asked. 'Can I see my son?'

'I'd like to see him, too,' Mrs Hallet declared, 'and I'm sure his great-grandmother would just love to see the newest addition to our family, wouldn't you, Rita?'

The ward clerk looked as though she would have preferred to have been force-fed poison, but she managed a tight-lipped nod.

'Of course you can see him,' Jess declared, 'but I have to warn you that you might find the sight of him a bit upsetting. He's been very ill, you see,' she added as Nicola looked from her to Brianna in panic. 'He had to have an operation yesterday, and though he's come through that well, he has a lot of tubes and wires attached to him to help him breathe.'

'You mean, he might…he could…die?' Nicola said, fresh tears welling in her eyes.

'No, he won't die,' Brianna said with difficulty. 'The tubes and wires are only temporary, a precaution.'

'And the important thing to remember is, under all the tubes and wires, he's still your son,' Jess said gently. 'He's still your baby.'

Your baby.

Not my baby, Brianna thought as Jess led the way out

of the staffroom, and she followed slowly. He was Nicola Hallet's baby, and she was happy about that—of course she was—because a baby should always be with its mother. It was the natural order of things, it was what was right.

'Are you OK?' Connor said the moment he saw her, his eyes worried, his face drawn.

'Of course I am,' she replied. 'Why wouldn't I be?'

'Brianna—'

She swept past him into the ward, her head held high, but, as she stood to one side of the incubator, and saw Mrs Hallet beam with clear pleasure at her grandson, and Nicola gaze down at him with such love in her eyes, she felt her heart twist inside her. Connor's eyes were fixed on her, she knew they were, but she couldn't meet his gaze, knew she would see sympathy there, and she didn't want to see sympathy, but when the baby stretched up one of his tiny hands towards his mother's face, she couldn't bear it. She just couldn't bear to be there, witnessing this reunion, and quietly she slipped out of the ward, needing to get away, to go anywhere, just so long as it was away.

'Brianna, wait!'

Connor had come after her, and she didn't want to see him, or hear his unease.

'You'll have to excuse me,' she said, turning her back on him, fast. 'I have things to do, paperwork—forms—to fill in…'

Quickly, she began to walk away from him, but he caught her by the elbow and steered her deliberately into the nurse unit manager's office.

'Brianna, sweetheart, you don't have to be brave,' he said, and she could see the anxiety in his eyes for her. 'I know how hard this must be for you.'

'It's not hard at all,' she said brightly. 'I'm fine, perfectly fine. It's great that Harry—Colin's—mother has come forward for him. Absolutely great.'

'She seems a very sweet girl,' he said carefully.

'And I'm sure she'll look after him perfectly well even though she's just sixteen,' she declared, picking up a piece of paper from his desk, then putting it down again, 'and it's not little Harry...' She bit her lip. '*Colin's* fault he'll have the great-grandmother from hell.'

'I think we can be sure Nicola's mother will tell Rita to back off in no uncertain terms.'

She nodded. 'Yes, of course she will, but...' She picked up the sheet of paper again. 'Connor, how can we be sure this girl is his mother? I mean, what proof do we have?'

'Jess recognised her as the girl who came in that day.'

'But that doesn't prove anything, does it?' she argued back. 'Just because she's the girl Jess saw doesn't mean—'

'Brianna, she's his mother, you know she is,' he interrupted gently, 'and, though she's very young, I think she has a sensible head on her shoulders, and her mother and father will help her, make sure she does right by the little boy.'

'Yes, of course they will,' she murmured. 'And Mrs Hallet looked nice. Don't you think she looked nice?' she added, all too aware she was talking too much, but if she stopped...if she stopped... 'And the Hallets have a farm, so Colin will have all those wonderful places to play in, just as I did when I was a child, and I'll see him occasionally, won't I—around and about in Penhally. Not often, of course, but I might see him sometimes—'

'Oh, Bree—'

'And it won't matter that he won't remember me,' she said on a sob, 'because that's as it should be. He'll have his real mother, and lots of aunts and uncles, and probably grandparents—'

'Bree, I'm so sorry,' Connor said, his heart breaking for her, 'so very, very sorry. I know you wanted him, had grown to care for him.'

'But I'm not his mother, am I?' she said, as tears began to roll down her cheeks. 'And a baby…a baby should always be with his mother. Except he did look so much…so very much like Harry, and now…and now…'

And Connor reached for her, and she stepped into his arms, and he held her tight, and didn't tell her not to cry, knew better now, and thanked God that the tears she wept into his shoulder weren't like the tears she'd shed for their own Harry. That these were tears of regret, tears for what could never be, what he suspected she'd always known, deep down, could never be, and yet had still hoped.

'I'm OK now,' she hiccuped when her tears were finally spent.

'You're sure?' he said anxiously, drying her face with his fingertips, scanning her eyes with concern.

'Yes,' she said, beginning to nod, then shook her head. 'No, I'm not, but I will be.'

'Honestly?' he said, and she manufactured a smile.

'Honestly.'

'I think we should go home,' he said, and she closed her eyes.

'I can't—I have another two hours of my shift to work.'

'I'll square it with Megan—she'll understand.'

Going home sounded good. Getting away from the unit for even a little while seemed even better.

'OK. All right,' she said.

Connor made for the door, then stopped. 'You will still be here when I get back, won't you?'

'I'm not going anywhere,' she said with a trembling smile. 'Not without you.'

And he smiled. A wide, comforting smile that warmed her bruised and battered heart.

'Give me two minutes,' he said. 'I won't be any longer.'

She hoped he wouldn't be. She didn't want Rita to suddenly appear. The ward clerk might have been a thorn in her side ever since she'd come to St Piran, but she could not find it in her to gloat over Rita's clear discomfiture, though she knew many of the hospital staff undoubtedly would. All she wanted was to go home, to have some peace and quiet to come to terms with Nicola's appearance, but peace turned out to be in short supply when Connor returned and they walked together down the stairs towards the exit.

The nearer they got to the ground floor, the more Brianna became aware of the sound of angry voices. Voices that seemed to be raised in unison, in something that sounded almost like a chant, and when she and Connor reached the entrance hall to the hospital she stopped dead.

The forecourt in front of the hospital was a seething mass of people. People of all ages and sexes who were carrying placards with the letters 'SOB' painted on them.

'What in the world…?' she began, as Connor let out a muttered oath. 'It looks like some kind of demonstration, but what on earth are people demonstrating about, and what does SOB mean?'

'Brianna, come back into the hospital,' Connor said quickly. 'I need to talk to you. My report…it's nowhere near completed yet. I still have lots of departments to assess, and what I've written is simply an initial recommendation, based on my first impressions, not a definitive view.'

'But, how would anyone know what you'd written?' she said in confusion. 'Not even the secretaries in Admin are good enough to read your mind.'

'My notes were on that memory card—the one I lost

or…' Connor came to a halt and frowned. Kennie Vernon was amongst the demonstrators, notebook in hand, and he smiled when he saw Connor, a smile that was triumphant, and Connor swore, long and low, and fluently. 'He must have taken it. It was in the staffroom with my laptop yesterday when he came in to see Brooke. That low-life reporter must have taken it.'

'But what did your notes say?' Brianna demanded, still confused. 'What do all these banners mean?'

'Bree, I'm sorry, those notes were private, no one was supposed to see them yet, and they're only my thoughts, suggestions…'

His voice trailed away into silence, and as she stared at him blankly the penny dropped, and her blankness gave way to anger. A seething, furious anger.

'SOB,' she said. 'It stands for Save Our Babies, doesn't it? You've recommended to the board that they shut down the neonatal intensive care unit.'

'Brianna, it's not definite yet—'

'But you've recommended it,' she repeated. 'You looked at our unit, and you had the…the callousness…the insensitivity…to actually say it wasn't doing a good job!'

'It's not a question of whether it's doing a good job or not,' he said defensively. 'The work that's done in the unit is second to none—I would never disagree with that—but I have to go by the statistics—figures. The unit in Plymouth can cater for double the amount of babies—'

'Cater?' she exclaimed. '*Cater?* Connor, we're not some sort of fast-food restaurant, we're a specialist nursing centre!'

'Brianna—'

'And if you shut us down it's not simply a case of saying, well, all the babies can go to Plymouth. What about the winter, when the roads are icy, or blocked with snow? What about the height of summer when the road is packed with slow-moving caravans and sightseeing tourists? That thirty-mile journey could take an hour—more!'

'If it's a real emergency you have a helicopter service—'

'Which could be out on another call when we need it, or grounded by ice or gale-force winds.'

'Brianna—'

'It's always been figures and numbers, for you, hasn't it?' she said furiously. 'Forget about what people—real people—want or need. Connor, can't you see that not everything can be neatly tied up in a balance sheet?'

'But it makes good medical as well as economic sense,' he protested. 'Can't you at least see that?'

It also meant something else, she realised. Something that was altogether much, much closer to home.

'There'll also be no nurse unit manager's job for me either, will there, if you shut us down?' she said icily. 'Is that why you're doing this, because you think if I don't have a job I'll come back to you?'

'Of course that isn't what I thought!' he exclaimed, anger darkening his face. 'Brianna, listen to me—'

'And to think I told Rita you'd never let personal bias influence your work,' she continued, fury plain in her voice. 'You took one look at Penhally, and St Piran, and thought dead-end places. You thought no way would I ever want to live here, so let's make sure Brianna can't either, and then she'll meekly come back with me to London.'

'That never occurred to me for a second,' he flared.

'Just like it didn't occur to you last night to tell me what you were planning to do with my unit,' she retorted. 'You let me think you'd changed, Connor. You made me think you cared—'

'I did—I do—'

'Then how can you even *think* of shutting down an

NICU?' she cried. 'It's where Harry spent his few hours of life, where all these babies I look after get a chance to live. OK, so we couldn't save Harry, but just because we couldn't it doesn't mean you should deny all these other babies that chance.'

'Brianna—'

'I want you out of my house when I get home tonight,' she said, her voice shaking with anger. 'I want you, and your posh designer suits, and your expensive shirts and shoes, and your damn, all-singing-all-dancing phone out of my house by the time I get home, and if they're not I'll dump the whole lot in my garden.'

'Can't we at least sit down and talk about this like sensible human beings?' he exclaimed. 'If you would just let me explain—'

'There's no need to,' she interrupted, 'because I already know what you are. You're a bastard, Connor. A complete and utter bastard.'

And she walked away from him, pushing her way through the demonstrators who had now spilled out of the forecourt and into the hospital foyer, only to discover her way barred by Kennie Vernon. Normally she would have walked straight past him, but this time she didn't. This time she stopped and, sensing a scoop, he pulled out his pen.

'Do you have a comment for me, Sister Flannigan, for our readers?'

Brianna glanced over her shoulder. Someone in the crowd had clearly recognised Connor because he had been surrounded by demonstrators, and was being heckled mercilessly.

'Yes, I have a comment to make,' she said, completely uncaring of what Admin might say when they saw her words on the front page of tomorrow's paper. 'I think even the idea of shutting down our NICU is an appalling one.

We have an excellent unit here. A unit that serves the needs of the local community, and I am fully behind this protest, and I wish the organisers well.'

And she made for the stairs, looking over her shoulder only once, when a great cheer went up. Someone had thrown an egg at Connor. An egg which had landed smack-bang on the front of his smart city suit. And her one thought as she headed back to the unit was she wished she'd had an egg because she would have thrown it, too.

CHAPTER SEVEN

'WE NEVER thought this day would come, Sister Flannigan.' Naomi Renwick beamed. 'To be finally taking Amy home...'

'And I've taken a photograph of her—for your graduation board,' Naomi's husband declared. 'So other mothers and fathers can see there truly can be light at the end of the tunnel.'

'It's a lovely picture,' Brianna said as she took the photograph Mr Renwick was holding out to her. 'Thank you very much.'

'We were hoping we might see Mr Monahan before we go,' Naomi said. 'He's been so supportive over this last month, always stopping by for a chat whenever my husband and I have visited Amy in the evening.'

'He has—he did?' Brianna said faintly. 'I...I didn't know that.'

'He's a nice bloke,' Mr Renwick observed, 'and he seemed quite taken with our Amy. As I said to him, you're clearly getting broody, Connor, so maybe you and Sister Flannigan should be thinking about having kids of your own soon.'

'And...and what did he say to that?' Brianna asked through a throat so tight it hurt.

'He just smiled,' Naomi replied. 'Look, I know he got

a lot of very bad press after his notes were published in the *Gazette*,' Amy's mother continued quickly as Brianna took a shaky breath, 'but we can honestly say your husband never had anything but praise for the unit when he was talking to us.'

Connor hadn't simply got bad press, Brianna remembered. The board had been forced to issue a statement declaring no decision had been made about any cuts to services, but nobody in the hospital had believed that. Everyone simply thought that if NICU couldn't be closed because of the public outcry, it only meant some other department would be shut down instead.

'Connor did say he would definitely see us and Amy before we left,' Mr Renwick said, 'and I told him we'd be collecting her at four o'clock, so maybe we could give him another few minutes?'

The couple didn't have to. The ward door had opened, and Connor appeared.

'You made it, Connor.' Mr Renwick beamed. 'We thought you might have forgotten, or been too busy.'

'I'd never be too busy for such a momentous occasion, and I most certainly wouldn't forget,' he replied.

And his gaze was fixed firmly on the Renwicks, Brianna noticed, but what had she expected? He'd tried to talk to her over the past five weeks, had left innumerable messages on her answering-machine, had once even come to her cottage, and she'd refused to open the door. She'd been so angry, so very angry. A part of her still was, and yet, as she gazed up at him, all she could think was this was his last day in the hospital. Tomorrow he would leave St Piran, and, when he left, their marriage would be finally, and irrevocably, be over.

'Sister Flannigan, can we take a photograph of you and Connor together?' Mr Renwick asked. 'It would be something to show Amy when she grows up. A picture of the husband-and-wife team who helped her parents so much.'

'I really think it should just be a photograph of Sister Flannigan,' Connor said quickly, but Naomi shook her head.

'I want the two of you together,' she said.

Which was fine in theory, Brianna thought, but not so fine in practice. Naomi clearly wanted a 'happy couple' photograph, and neither of them fitted that bill any more.

'Connor, can't you at least put your arm around her?' Naomi protested. 'You're standing there looking like she's a complete stranger, and Sister Flannigan, a smile would be nice. I don't want Amy looking at this photograph in years to come and saying, "Yikes, they look grim", and I'm sure you don't want a picture of yourselves looking like a pair of stuffed dummies.'

And Connor dutifully put his arm around her, and Brianna forced herself to smile, and tried very hard not to cry.

All the dreams she'd had ten years ago on their wedding day. All the plans she'd made, the hopes she'd had, and now the last photograph of them together would be of her wearing a manufactured smile, and him not even attempting to smile at all.

Tell him you don't want him to go, her heart whispered. Tell him you want him to stay here, to try to make your marriage work.

But she couldn't. Connor and Cornwall were as compatible as cheese and gravy, and she couldn't go back to London with him. She knew she would just shrivel up and die in the city so, when the Renwicks carried their daughter out of the ward, she kept her gaze firmly fixed on them, and only let out the breath she knew she'd been holding when she heard the ward door shut.

'Colin's had three full bottles today,' Nicola Hallet said proudly as Brianna slowly walked past her. 'Dr Phillips said if he keeps on progressing like this she'll be recommending he's moved out of NICU and into Special Care, and after that…' Nicola beamed. 'Home. I'll finally be able to take him home.'

'That's terrific news, Nicola,' Brianna said, meaning it.

Young though the teenager might be, Nicola was proving to be an excellent, and completely devoted, mother, coming in every day to feed and bathe her son, and to talk and play with him.

'Your husband said he wants me to keep in touch with him, to let him know how Colin is, when he goes back to London,' Nicola continued, gazing fondly down at her son. 'Wasn't that kind of him?'

'Very kind,' Brianna said unevenly. 'When…when did he say all this?'

'On one of his visits to the unit,' Nicola replied. 'He's been coming here a lot in the evening.'

Who else had Connor been talking to? Brianna wondered, taking a shaky breath. First the Renwicks, and now Nicola, but *why*? What had drawn him back here, apparently night after night?

'Nicola—'

'How's my favourite boy in all the world?' Jess asked with a smile as she joined them.

'Dr Phillips said she's thinking of moving Colin to Special Care next week,' Nicola answered.

'That's wonderful news,' the counsellor declared, then glanced across at Brianna. 'Have you a moment?'

'Something wrong?' Brianna asked as she followed Jess across the ward, and the counsellor shook her head.

'I passed Connor in the corridor on my way in, and he said he'd like a word with you, if you've time.'

He wanted to say goodbye, Brianna realised, and she didn't want to say goodbye, didn't think her heart could take that.

'I'm afraid I'm rather busy at the moment,' she lied, and Jess sighed.

'Brianna, talk to him,' she said softly. 'What harm can it do just to talk to him?'

'Jess, what is there left for us to say that we haven't already said?' Brianna said sadly. 'I think a clean break, with no goodbyes, is best.'

'And you truly believe that?' Jess said with eyes that saw too much.

'Jess, just leave it, OK?'

'But, Brianna—'

She didn't give the counsellor time to finish. Instead, she walked over to one of the monitors, and swallowed hard. If talking to Connor would have changed anything, she would have done it in a minute, but it wouldn't change anything, she knew it wouldn't.

Determinedly, she picked up the pile of files stacked on the nurses' work station. She should have tackled them days ago, but she'd been so tired recently. Tired and un-characteristically weepy, and she bit her lip. Maybe she should never have accepted the nurse unit manager's job. Maybe she just wasn't up to it, and she ought to simply tell Mr Brooke so.

'Brianna?'

She glanced over her shoulder to see Megan standing behind her.

'I've just passed Connor in the corridor,' the paediatric specialist registrar declared, 'and he said he'd like—'

'A word with me,' Brianna finished for her. 'Yes, I know.'

'I can hold the fort for you here, if you want. It would be no trouble.'

'Look, what is this?' Brianna exclaimed, taking refuge in anger. 'If it's not you, it's Jess, trying to push me out the door to talk to him.'

'I just thought that, as this is his last day…'

'I know what you thought,' Brianna said tightly, 'and, trust me, it isn't going to happen.'

'Brianna, don't you think you should at least let him say what he wants to say?' Megan said, her eyes concerned. 'You can tear him to shreds afterwards if you want, but, when he's been the one continually holding out the olive branch, couldn't you at least meet him halfway and hear him out?'

'Yeah, right. Like you do with Josh, you mean?' Brianna snapped. 'I can't say I've seen any signs of that.'

Megan flushed scarlet, opened her mouth, then closed it again tightly.

'OK, if that's how you feel,' she said, 'but I'm not going out there to tell him you won't see him. You can do that yourself, or you can leave him standing in the corridor waiting for hours in the hope you might change your mind. Your choice.'

'Megan—'

The paediatric specialist registrar had walked away, and Brianna started after her, then stopped. What in the world was happening to her? Megan and Jess both meant well, she knew they did, and yet she'd chewed their heads off. Chewed the heads off the two women she'd always thought of as friends, and she wanted to burst into tears again, and she really had to stop wanting to burst into tears.

Go and see him, a little voice whispered at the back of her mind. *You want to, you know you do, so go and see him.*

I can't, her heart cried. I can't. I don't want to say goodbye.

It will be the last time you ever see him, the little voice whispered. *The last time you'll ever see his face.* And before she was even aware she was moving, she was out in the corridor and he was there, waiting for her.

'Thanks for agreeing to see me,' he said.

Lord, but he looked so nervous, so awkward and un-comfortable, totally unlike her normally super-confident husband.

'Megan and Jess, seemed to think it was important,' she replied, only to realise, too late, just how awful her words sounded, as though her friends might care about him but she did not. 'I mean—'

'I thought you should know what's in my report to the board before it becomes common knowledge tomorrow,' he interrupted.

'You don't have to tell me the details,' she said quickly. 'I don't need to know before anyone else does.'

'Yes, you do,' he insisted. 'I've recommended no depart-ments, or wards, should be shut.'

She blinked. 'None?'

'I've had a lot of time to think over this past month,' he declared with a rueful half-smile, 'and I've realised you were right. Not everything can be measured on a balance sheet.'

'But, if you don't suggest any cuts, won't the board simply bring in someone else to audit us?' she protested.

'They need to save money, and won't they reason that if you can't find a solution then maybe somebody else might?'

'I've shown them how they can save money,' he replied. 'I've recommended cancelling the new, all-singing, all-dancing computer system they've ordered. Their old computer system—with some modifications—is more than up to the task.'

'Right.' She nodded.

He backed up a step. 'Well…that's all I wanted to tell you, so…'

He was going and, as she stared up at him, saw how careworn he looked, how very weary, she knew she still loved him. Despite everything he'd done, despite everything that had happened, she still loved him, and surely there had to be some way back for them, some way they could still be together?

'Connor…'

He stopped, and something that looked almost like hope stirred in his deep blue eyes. 'Yes?'

'I just wanted to say—you know—thank you,' she said awkwardly. 'On behalf of the parents, and the babies, I mean,' she added.

'That's OK,' he muttered.

Oh, Lord, but why had she said that? She'd always been the one who'd accused him of not talking, of not saying what he was really thinking, and now she couldn't seem to find the right words.

'You'll be going back to London tomorrow?' she said desperately.

'Not immediately,' he replied. 'I thought I might stay on here for a little while, have a holiday.'

Despite herself, her lips curved.

'You're not going to find much to do in Penhally in

April,' she observed, and saw an answering, hesitant, smile appear on his lips.

'Maybe I'll take up beachcombing,' he said. 'How's the new job going?'

'Tiring,' she admitted. 'I hadn't realised before just how much paperwork was involved.'

'You look tired,' he observed. 'Just don't overdo it, OK? I've had to learn the hard way that there's more to life than work.'

He's given you an opening, she thought, so use it. Use it now, but she didn't get a chance to.

'How's Rita?' he continued, and, when she rolled her eyes, he laughed. 'That good, eh?'

'She was pretty subdued for about a week, but she bounced right back again pretty quickly. As she said to me, "Sister Flannigan, the Bible does say that charity begins at home, so I'd hardly be a good Christian if I didn't find it in me to forgive my own granddaughter's transgressions."'

'She actually said that?' Connor gasped, and Brianna nodded.

'Yup, she did. I'm afraid nothing keeps our Rita down for long.'

'You know, in a weird way, I think I'm going to miss her,' he observed. 'Of course, it's going to be in a *very* weird way.'

Brianna laughed and, as he half turned, clearly thinking their conversation was over, she took a step forward.

'The Renwicks told me you've been visiting the unit in the evening,' she said. 'Nicola said you've been talking to her, too.'

'They're a nice couple, and she's a sweet kid, so...' His shoulders lifted awkwardly.

'But why, Connor?' she asked. 'Your assessment of

NICU was over weeks ago, so why did you keep coming back here?'

To her surprise, a deep tide of colour crept over her husband's cheeks.

'It's stupid—silly,' he muttered. 'Not worth talking about.'

'Tell me,' she pressed.

'You'll think I'm crazy.'

'Just tell me,' she protested, and saw him take a deep breath.

'Because it's where you work, and being in the unit... Sometimes I caught a hint of the soap you use, and it made me feel...close to you again, as though I was still a part of your life.'

Tears welled in her eyes. 'Oh, Connor—'

'Told you it was stupid, didn't I?' he said awkwardly, and she shook her head.

'No,' she replied with difficulty. 'I don't think it's stupid at all.'

'I'd better go,' he said again. 'I've taken up more than enough of your time.'

She put out her hand quickly.

'This holiday you're taking,' she said hesitantly. 'It seems like such a waste of money for you to stay in a hotel. You...you could move back into my cottage tomorrow, if you want. I mean, it would give us more time to talk,' she continued, feeling her cheeks beginning to darken as he stared at her, his face expressionless. 'And I...I would very much like for us to talk some more, if...if you'd like to, that is?'

A smile curved the corners of his mouth. A smile that grew, and grew.

'I would like that very much indeed,' he said, and she smiled in return, a suddenly shy, self-conscious smile.

'I'd better get back to work,' she said, 'otherwise they'll be sending out a search party for me.'

He nodded, and she turned, but she must have turned too fast because a wave of giddiness swept over her, and if Connor hadn't caught her she would have fallen.

'Are you OK?' he said anxiously.

'Rush of blood to the head, that's all,' she said, wishing the walls in the corridor would stop moving.

'You're sure?' he pressed. 'Hell, Brianna, you're chalk-white.'

'I'm fine—just fine,' she said shakily, taking several deep breaths. 'I shouldn't have skipped breakfast this morning, but I felt a bit queasy.'

'You'll have breakfast every morning when I move back in, and no arguments,' he said firmly, and she laughed.

'Going to be the flatmate from hell, are you?' she said, and he smiled but she could see his eyes were still concerned.

'When it comes to your health, you bet I am,' he declared.

She still felt slightly sick, and giddy, she realised as she walked away from him back into the ward, and it was weird. She didn't get sick—never had done. It had always been Connor who contracted every cold or infection going. She'd used to laugh, and tell him he could be the one-stop shop for medical students practising their skills, and he hadn't appreciated the joke. The only time she'd ever felt sick…

She came to a halt in the middle of the ward, her heart suddenly racing. The only time she'd ever felt sick had been when she'd been expecting Harry. The only time her emotions had been all over the place, as they were right now, had been when she'd been pregnant with Harry.

'No,' she whispered, as she desperately tried to count

back to the night when she and Connor had made love. 'I can't be. I can't.'

But she could.

Keep calm, she told herself, don't panic, keep calm. You could simply be late. You've only missed one period, and stress can do that. It took seven years for you to conceive Harry so the odds on you conceiving in one night are minuscule.

But not impossible.

'Chris, I just need to slip out for a moment,' she said, hoping her voice didn't sound nearly as strained as she thought it did.

It couldn't have done because the staff nurse simply nodded vaguely, and quickly Brianna left the unit and headed for Gynae.

No matter how long she stared at the thin blue lines they didn't go away. She'd sneaked three pregnancy kits out of Gynae, had been determined to leave nothing to chance, and each and every one of the kits said the same thing. She was pregnant.

'Brianna, are you in there?' Megan called, from outside the staffroom toilet.

'Yes…I'm here,' she managed to say.

'A and E have phoned. Four-month-old on its way to us. Mother seriously injured in a car crash, baby looks to have nothing more than minor lesions but they want us to check him out.'

And I don't want to do this, Brianna thought, squeezing her eyes shut. I can't deal with this, not right now, but she knew she must.

'I'll be out in a minute,' she said, and, when she heard Megan's footsteps fading away, she stared at the pregnancy kits on the floor in front of her.

One pregnancy test could get it wrong, but it was impossible for three to give the wrong result. A baby was growing inside her, and no amount of staring at the kits would alter that. No amount of willing the results to be different would change them, and stiffly she got to her feet, and even more stiffly walked out of the toilet, down the corridor, and into the ward.

The heat enveloped her instantly, but it didn't comfort her as it normally did. All she could see were the IV lines, tubes and incubators. All she could hear was the rasping sound of the ventilators, the constant bleep of the monitors, and in seven months' time, if she didn't go full term, as she hadn't before, she'd be back in here, not as a nurse but as a mother. A mother whose child's life would be attached to all those tubes and wires. A mother whose child would be clinging to life. A sob broke from her.

'Brianna, what's wrong?'

Megan was standing in front of her, her eyes full of concern, and Brianna shook her head.

'I have to get out of here.'

'But—'

'I can't bear this, I can't!' Brianna exclaimed, all too aware that Chris was gazing at her open-mouthed, Mr Brooke looked stunned, and Josh...

He was there, too, and he was walking towards her, worry and confusion written all over his face, and she turned and ran. Out of the ward, out of the unit, not knowing know where she was going, not even caring, just so long as she got away.

'Brianna, wait up a moment!'

She didn't want to wait as she heard Megan running after her. She was going to have wait for the next eight months, endure eight whole months of fear, and she pressed her fist against her mouth hard as another sob came from her.

'Brianna, what's happened? What's wrong?'

Megan had caught up with her, was trying to steer her into the on-call room, and she tried to pull herself free, but the paediatric specialist registrar was a lot stronger than she looked.

'Megan, let me go,' she said, her voice raw. 'Please, just let me go.'

'No way,' her friend replied. 'You're clearly very upset. Shall I get Connor? I can phone him—'

'No—no—don't get him!' Brianna begged. 'Please, don't get him!'

'Then tell me what's wrong, what's happened, because I swear I'll phone him if you don't,' Megan replied, her eyes dark with anxiety.

Slowly, Brianna went into the on-call room, and sat down heavily on the bed.

'I… Oh, God, Megan. I'm pregnant.'

The specialist paediatric registrar stared at her silently for a heartbeat, then sat down beside her.

'And I take it this is not good news?' she said gently.

'It's the worst news,' Brianna cried. 'The very worst news in the world!'

Megan's eyes darkened with an expression Brianna didn't understand, then she cleared her throat.

'The baby…is it Connor's?' she asked hesitantly, and when Brianna nodded she sighed. 'Look, I know you're not exactly on speaking terms with him at the moment, but you told me just a few weeks ago that you loved him, and maybe you can resolve whatever's driven you apart, and even if you can't, lots of women are single mothers—'

'I know,' Brianna interrupted. 'I know all that, but it isn't that simple, Megan, I wish to God it was. Three years ago Connor and I…we had a child. We'd been trying for a baby for seven years, and when I discovered I was pregnant it was…' She took an uneven breath. 'It was like having all of my birthdays and Christmases in one go.'

'What happened?' Megan asked, her eyes fixed on her.

'I must have had one of the worst pregnancies ever,' Brianna replied. 'I was sick the whole time, but I didn't care. I used to talk to him, Megan. All the time I'd talk to the baby, tell him what I was doing, what I could see, and tell him how…' Tears spilled over her cheeks, and she didn't rub them away. 'How he was going to be the most loved baby in the whole world, and when he was born… Connor—he says he looked like me, but he didn't. He looked like him, and he died, Megan. He only lived for twelve hours, and then my beautiful, precious son died.'

'Oh, Brianna, I am so sorry,' Megan declared, her own eyes filling, 'and discovering you're pregnant again… You must be scared to death, but just because your son died doesn't mean every other baby you have will die, too.'

'He had an inherited heart condition, Megan, and you know what that means. It means there's a very strong likelihood it will happen again.'

'Brianna, listen to me—'

'Why?' Brianna hurled at her. 'What's the point? You don't understand—you can't. You've never given birth to a child and been forced to watch him die. You've never watched your baby slowly slip away from you, knowing there was nothing you could to stop it.'

'I have.'

Brianna's eyes flew to her friend's, and she saw such an unutterable pain there that for a moment she forgot her own despair.

'You had a baby?' she whispered.

'A son, like you,' Megan replied, her voice low, but there was no mistaking the heartache in it. 'He was born eight years ago when I was a student doctor. His father was a doctor, too, working in the same hospital as me, and he was so handsome, Brianna. Handsome, and charming, and such fun, and I…' She closed her eyes. 'Even though he never seemed to notice me, I guess I was a little in love with him right from the first moment I saw him.'

'You're…you're talking about Josh, aren't you?' Brianna said hesitantly, and Megan nodded.

'I always thought I was too quiet for him, too studious, and then…' She took a breath. 'I went to a party, and he was there, and suddenly he seemed very interested in me, and…' A tear ran down the paediatric specialist registrar's cheek, and she brushed it away. 'It wasn't a one-night stand, Brianna, not for me. I thought it was the start of something special, but…'

'He walked away when he discovered you were pregnant?' Brianna said tentatively, and Megan laughed.

A harsh, bitter laugh that made Brianna wince.

'I didn't even get the chance to tell him I was pregnant. We were supposed to meet up the next day, and he stood me up, and when I saw him a few days later, he blanked me. He just walked straight past me as though he'd never met me, far less made love to me.'

'Oh, Megan—'

'When I discovered I was pregnant, my career was just taking off, and I thought, I can't give this baby a home. I can't give him the attention he deserves, so I was going to have an abortion until I saw the scan. When I saw this tiny figure inside me…' She shook her head. 'This tiny, oh, so perfect little human being inside me…'

'You couldn't go through with it.'

'He was my baby, Brianna, my little boy, and even if his father didn't want him, I did, and then…' Megan took a deep breath, and Brianna could see her friend's lips were trembling. 'I collapsed in the street when I was twenty-three weeks pregnant. Placental abruption, that's what the doctor in A and E said, and I was bleeding out, and I could hear someone shouting, "She has to be saved. The baby can't be saved, but we can save her", and I didn't want them to save me. I…' A sob escaped her. 'I just wanted to die, to be with my son, but they didn't let me die. They performed a complete hysterectomy, which means I can't ever have any more children.'

'Oh, Megan,' Brianna cried. 'I am sorry…so, so sorry.'

'I have relived that day so many times, Brianna,' Megan said, her voice shaking. 'Wondered so often if maybe Stephen knew I'd considered having an abortion, and, because he thought I didn't want him, he decided I was better off without him, but I wasn't. I wasn't.'

'But, having been through all that, having suffered the death of a child, can't you see why I can't face this again?' Brianna insisted. 'Can't you understand that I can't carry a child, grow to love it, and then have that baby die, too?'

'Brianna, statistically, the odds that everything might be all right—'

'*Might* be—*could* be. Megan I don't want *might*,' Brianna protested. 'I don't want *could*. I want you to tell me this baby will live!'

'I can't promise you that—no one can,' Megan replied. 'Brianna—'

She'd already got jerkily to her feet.

'I want to go home, Megan. I just want to get away from here, and go home.'

'But, Brianna…'

Her friend was already heading out of the on-call room, and for a moment Megan stared indecisively after her, then pulled her mobile phone from her pocket and dialled quickly.

'Pick up your phone, Connor,' she muttered. 'This is important, so pick up your damn phone!'

But he didn't. She'd reached his voice mail, and the last thing she wanted was his voice mail, but she left a message anyway, and then she left the on-call room only to stop dead. Josh was standing outside in the corridor, and his face told her everything.

'You heard,' she said flatly, and, when he nodded she shrugged, though her eyes were dark with shadows. 'There's no need to look quite so shocked. It's not as though you didn't already know about Stephen, and my hysterectomy.'

'Megan—'

She didn't let him finish. She simply walked back into the duty room and slammed the door, but he came in after her.

'Megan, if I could have saved Stephen, I would,' Josh said hoarsely. 'But he was too little, too premature, you know he was, and if we hadn't carried out the hysterectomy, you would have *died*, and I couldn't have borne that. Losing you as well as my son—'

'Are you asking me to believe you *cared*?' she demanded, her voice hard. 'If you are, then it's too little, too late.'

'Megan, listen to me,' he begged, his face white. 'You cannot possibly hate me more than I hate myself right now. When I held Stephen in my hands for those few brief moments, when I saw he wasn't breathing, knew he would never breathe—'

'Don't, Josh,' she protested, her face stricken, 'please *don't*—'

'And they rushed you to Theatre, and you were losing so much blood—'

'If you cared that much then why did you walk away from me?' she cried, her voice cracking. 'I thought we'd meant something to one another that night, and yet you didn't even turn up the next day as we'd arranged.'

'I was scared, Megan. My father...' He shook his head. 'He hurt my mother time and time again with his affairs, and yet she kept on taking him back, and taking him back, and I thought, if that's love, I want none of it. If that's what giving your heart means, I can't do that, so all my life I've refused to allow myself to get too close to anyone for fear I'd hurt them, or they'd hurt me.'

'And yet you married Rebecca,' she pointed out, and he bit his lip.

'I should never have done that—I see that now—but I married her because I was lonely. I married her because I was unhappy, and I married her because...' He sucked in an uneven breath. 'She wanted so little from me. I'm ashamed to admit that—I should never have married her when all I felt for her was a liking—but I thought she was happy. I told myself she was, but she wasn't.'

'Josh—'

'Megan, I have ruined three lives,' he said desolately. 'Yours, my wife's, my own, and though I deserve everything I've got—my wife walking out on me, you hating me—neither you nor Rebecca deserve the pain I've inflicted on you both.'

'I don't hate you,' Megan said, her voice trembling. 'I may have once, a long time ago. I may even have wished you'd never come back into my life, but I don't hate you. I don't think I ever could.'

'I know I can never make it up to you,' he said. 'I know I can never expect you to forgive me, or to care for me the way I care for you—'

'You care for me?' she interrupted, and he smiled, a lopsided, crooked smile.

'I realise now, though it's too late, that I always have, and I just want to say I'm sorry. I know that's a pathetic thing to say,' he continued, as a tear trickled down Megan's cheek, 'a completely inadequate thing to say, and I wish there were bigger words, better words I could use to convince you I truly am sorry for all the pain and heartache I've caused you, but there aren't.'

'I don't need bigger or better words,' she said on a sob. 'Those words are enough.'

'Are you saying…?' His eyes met hers, and he swallowed hard. 'Are you saying that maybe…maybe you could learn to care for me again?'

'Josh, I always have,' she said simply, 'and, God help me, I think I always will.'

And when he hesitantly held out his arms to her she walked straight into them, and when he kissed her it was as though the last eight years had never been. As though all the heartache and pain they'd both endured had never happened. And he'd said he'd cared for her. OK, so he hadn't said the 'L' word, but she knew he meant the 'L' word, he truly did, and the shiver she felt when she heard the lonely wail of an approaching ambulance, a wail that sounded so like a lost soul crying for the happiness it could never have, meant nothing. It didn't, she told herself, so when he deepened his kiss, held her even closer, moulded his body to hers, and she felt herself melting, and dissolving in his heat, she didn't stop him when he stretched behind him, and turned the lock on the on-duty call-room door.

* * *

Brianna's house was in complete darkness when Connor reached it, and if it hadn't been for her car parked outside he would have thought she wasn't home.

'Brianna needs you,' Megan had said, sounding frantic on his voice mail. 'She's gone home, and she really needs you, Connor.'

He'd driven like a maniac along the narrow Cornish roads, broken the speed limit the whole way, and now...

Hesitantly, he tried the front door, and it opened immediately. Was that good, or bad? He didn't know, and even more hesitantly he walked down the hall to the sitting room. The room was in darkness, just like the rest of the house, but moonlight was streaming through the window and he could just about make Brianna out, sitting motionless and hunched on the sofa.

'You know, you really should lock your front door,' he said, switching on one of the table lamps. 'I could have been anyone. A burglar, a serial killer, a door-to-door salesman trying to sell you a hundred and one things you never ever wanted.'

She didn't so much as turn her head, and he shivered. The room was freezing, and quickly he switched on the gas fire, and watched the fake flames spring to life, before turning back to her.

Had she moved at all? He didn't think she had.

'I expect I'm the last person in the world you want to see,' he said, walking over to the sofa and sitting down beside her, hoping to at least provoke a response, but he didn't. 'Megan rang me. She was worried about you.'

Still she didn't move, and tentatively he reached out, and took her hand in his. Lord, but her fingers felt like ice, and the shiver he'd felt earlier became more pronounced.

'Has something happened at the hospital?' he asked, wishing she would look at him, say something, anything.

'Has someone upset you, or is it one of the babies? Has one of the babies become very ill?'

Still she said nothing, and he gripped her hand tighter.

'Bree, for God's sake, say something, because you're scaring the hell out of me,' he said, and she was. 'Are you ill? You had that giddy spell earlier—is it something to do with that, and there's something wrong with you? Look, whatever it is, we can deal with it. I'm not going to walk away, I'm not going to leave you—'

'I'm pregnant.'

Her voice was so low, he wasn't sure he'd heard her correctly, and he half shook his head.

'I'm sorry, but did you just say…?'

'I'm pregnant, Connor,' she said dully. 'The night little Colin Hallet had his op, when we made love, I must have conceived a baby then.'

'But that's…' His face lit up. 'Oh, Bree, that's wonderful news, the very best of news.'

Her head snapped round to his.

'*Wonderful* news—*the very best* of news?' she cried. 'I don't want to be pregnant, Connor. Can't you understand, *I don't want to be pregnant*!'

'Bree, I know this is a shock, something you never planned,' he declared, putting his hands on her shoulders, 'but you're going to have a baby—*a baby*—and it's what you always wanted, and if…' His face twisted slightly. 'If you don't want me in your life to share this with you, I'll understand. All I'll ask of you is that you let me sometimes be there, for the child.'

'What if it dies?' she exclaimed, getting jerkily to her feet, her face white, her eyes desperate. 'What if this baby dies, too, Connor? Before—because of my job—I knew things could sometimes go wrong, but I only knew it in an abstract way, something that happened to other people, not to me, but it *has* happened to me, and it could happen again—we both know it could. Even if I do all the right things, even if I never take any risks, just like I didn't with Harry, it could happen again. This baby could have the same inherited heart defect, and it could die!'

'It might not,' he said, reaching for her only to see her evade him, 'and if it does we'll face it together.'

'That's easy for you to say,' she said, a tear running down her cheek, and she dashed it away. 'You won't be able to feel him, or her, moving inside you. You won't lie awake at night, thinking he hasn't moved in a little while, and does that mean he's not alive any more. You were right about Nicola's baby. I wanted him because he had no one. I wanted him because he looked so like our Harry, but I also wanted him because...' Another tear trickled down her cheek and she let it fall. 'He was *whole*, Connor, he was going to live, and to have to wait to find out if this baby...'

'So, you're going to have an abortion?' he said, watching her face. 'You're going to abort this baby, not even give it a chance to live, is that it?'

She stared at him, her mouth working soundlessly for a moment, then before he knew what was happening she was standing in front of him, pounding his chest with her fists.

'How can you say that?' she cried, hitting him with every word she spoke. 'How can you even think I'd kill my child? Of course I would never kill my child, never, *never*!'

'I know,' he said, quickly catching her wrists with his hands. 'Brianna, I *know* you wouldn't, and that's why the only thing you can do is to go on with this, and we can face it together, we can do it together, if...' He searched her face. 'You want me in your life, that is? I know I've made mistakes,' he continued as she tried to interrupt. 'I know I've got things wrong, but I have never ever stopped loving you.'

'And I haven't ever stopped loving you,' she said brokenly. 'I think…maybe…we just sort of lost one another somehow along the way, but I am so scared, Connor, so scared. If this baby dies, too…'

'I'm scared, too,' he admitted, taking her into his arms, and holding her tight. 'In the past, I always thought I had control over my life, my future, but now I know that was nothing but an illusion, that none of us have any control, that all we can do is hold onto one another through the good times, and the bad, and pray and hope.'

'I want certainty, not hope,' she sobbed into his chest. 'I want to know for sure, not have to pray.'

He tilted her head back so she had to look at him.

'I know, and I think that's what we all want, but life isn't like that. For such a very long time I thought, Why my son, why did this have to happen to my son? But now I know there is no answer to that. When Harry died—'

'You said the word,' she interrupted. 'Do you realise that's the first time you've ever said the word?'

'I couldn't say it before, because saying it…' Connor swallowed hard. 'It made it so final, so irrevocable. It meant I had to accept he was never, ever coming back.'

'And he isn't, is he?' she said, and Connor shook his head, a muscle in his jaw quivering.

'No, but do you remember when they took him off the life-support machine, and you were holding him in your arms, and I had one of his tiny hands in mine…? Do you remember him opening his eyes, and looking at us before he died?'

She nodded with difficulty. 'I remember.'

'I think now he was saying, "I love you both, and I know

you love me, but I have to go now. I can't stay with you any longer."'

'Oh, Connor...'

'Brianna, there was a time when I thought I couldn't face going on without him,' he said shakily, as tears spilled down her cheeks. 'I couldn't see any future without him, but he's gone on without us, and we have to go on without him. We won't ever forget him—we can't, not ever—and he will always have a treasured place in our hearts, but we have to look forward and not back.'

'I can't go back to London with you,' she said quickly. 'I know you love the city, but I love it here.'

'We're staying here. We might need to look for a bigger house once the baby comes, unless your landlord will let us build an extension, but we're staying in Penhally.'

'But you'll be so miserable,' she protested, 'and where would you work?'

'I would never be miserable with you beside me,' he said, willing her to believe him, 'and I've already got a job in St Piran.'

'You've got a job?' she said, and he smiled.

'The hospital board want me to be their financial advisor.'

'And you were offered this job, and accepted it, and never told me?' she said in confusion.

'I knew you didn't want to see me, to talk to me,' he said, his voice low, 'but I hoped, if I stayed here...' He lifted his shoulders awkwardly. 'Maybe in time you might grow to love me again.'

'I do, I always have, but...' She tried to stop her lips from trembling, but she couldn't. 'Will the baby be all right this time, Connor?'

He cupped her face in his hands, his blue eyes holding hers.

'I don't know, but whatever happens we're in this together. No matter what the future brings, we will *always*
face it together.'

EPILOGUE

'AND how is my gorgeous wife this morning?'

'Your gorgeous wife feels like a barrage balloon that is about to burst.' Brianna sighed as she eased herself out of her seat.

'Back still sore?' Connor said sympathetically, coming up behind her and rubbing it gently.

'It must be the way I was sleeping—or rather not sleeping—last night,' she replied ruefully. 'I just couldn't get comfortable.'

'I'm not surprised.' Connor grinned, sliding his hands round to caress her swollen stomach. 'With two little munchkins in there, and only two weeks left until your due date, they're probably finding it a bit crowded.'

Brianna grimaced. 'Judging by how much they're kicking, that could be true.'

'Maybe they're both boys?' Connor exclaimed. 'Destined to be future world-class football players.'

Brianna closed her eyes. 'I just want them both to be all right.'

His arms tightened round her. 'They will be. Trust me.'

It wasn't a question of trust, she thought as she let her head fall back against his chest. It was a question now of luck, of the odds being stacked not once, but twice in their favour, and she didn't even want to think about what the chances of that happening might be.

'Stop worrying,' Connor said softly, clearly reading her mind, and she tried to smile, but it was hard.

She'd had a scan at twelve weeks, which had revealed she was expecting twins, but she'd refused to go for any more tests. She was more than happy to let the GP in Penhally regularly check her blood pressure, and to keep making sure there were still two little heartbeats, but she'd point blank refused to have any other kind of test, and Connor had backed her all the way.

'We'll deal with whatever happens when we have to,' he had told the GP, and, though the doctor hadn't been happy, he'd said no more.

'I was just thinking,' Connor continued hesitantly. 'Given that we're shortly going to be having two little babies in our home, are you quite sure you don't want the baby shower Jess and Megan want to throw for you?'

'Tell them I'm really touched, but no,' Brianna replied. 'I know everyone thinks I'm stupid, but...'

'You don't want to tempt fate,' Connor finished for her. 'Understood, though you do realise our children's first beds are going to be a couple of drawers because you won't even let me buy cots?'

'Connor—'

'And I'm sure they'll love the drawers,' he said, planting a kiss on the top of her head, then releasing her. 'I won't be late home tonight. I want to get the last of the onions, and carrots out of the ground before winter really sets in.'

She shook her head, and laughed. 'You and your vegetables. You'll be wanting us to buy chickens next.'

'Been reading my mind, have you?' He grinned, and she laughed again.

He'd taken to country living with an enthusiasm that

had amazed her. Never would she have thought her city-loving husband would have spent all of his spare time in the garden, creating a vegetable patch, but he had.

'No regrets?' she said. 'About living so far away from everything here in Cornwall?'

'Not a one. Everything I want is here.' He cupped her cheek, his blue eyes soft. 'I was just too blind and stupid to see it before.'

'And you're going to be late,' she said, catching sight of the kitchen clock. 'Give my best to the troops on the front line.'

'I will.' He nodded. 'You have my number in case you need me?'

She rolled her eyes.

'Connor, your number is the same number it was eight months ago, so get out of here.'

He turned to go, then came back, and took her in his arms. 'Have I told you this morning that I love you?'

'Twice.' She chuckled, as he kissed her. 'Though how you can love me when I look like a blob…'

'You have never looked more beautiful,' he said huskily, and her eyes filled.

'Lord, being pregnant isn't half playing havoc with my emotions,' she said tremulously. 'Now, will you *please* get out of here before I have to call the board and tell them their financial adviser is a fruitcake?'

'They already know that,' he replied, bending his head, clearly intent on kissing her again, and she fended him off.

'*Go!*'

She could hear him laughing as he went down the drive, and, when he drove away, she smiled as she absently rubbed her back. She hadn't ever been this happy, not even back in Killarney, and her pregnancy had been so much easier this time. She'd actually felt well instead of wretched, and all she needed now was...

'No,' she told the kettle as she made herself a cup of coffee. 'No thinking about what's going to happen in two weeks' time. Connor said it was forbidden.'

Which didn't mean she didn't constantly think about it, she realised as she drank her coffee. The nearer her due date loomed, the more frightened she was becoming.

'I'd much rather the two of you just stayed in there,' she told her bump. 'Where you're safe.'

One of the inhabitants of the bump kicked, and she winced slightly.

'I know, I know,' she said. 'You're eager to see the world, but stay where you are. You've only two more weeks to wait, and I have this laundry to do. Ninety-nine per cent of which,' she continued wryly as she bent to pick up the wash basket, 'appears to consist of your father's shirts, but I promise you I'll wean him out of his city suits one day.'

But not right now, she thought as a pain suddenly shot through her, and as she doubled up she felt something wet and warm trickle down her legs.

No! her mind exclaimed as she stared down and saw a bloody show among the liquid on the floor. Not now. She couldn't be going into labour now. It was too soon, too soon, and she took a deep breath and clutched the kitchen table tight, but the pain in her back was getting worse, a lot worse, and frantically she scrabbled for her mobile and dialled Connor's number.

He answered almost immediately, and she could hear the sound of traffic in the background which meant he had approached the town of St Piran.

'Connor Monahan here,' he declared cheerfully. 'World-renowned but also very modest financial advisor to St Piran Hospital, grower of the best onions in Cornwall, and lucky enough to be married to the most beautiful woman in the entire world, and, yes, I am remembering you want me to pick up some milk before I come home tonight.'

'Connor…' She struggled to keep her voice calm, but it didn't work. 'Connor, my waters have broken.'

For a second there was complete silence down the phone, then she heard him exhale, and the sound of his car accelerating.

'I'm on my way back. Stay where you are. Don't move.'

She wasn't going to, she thought as the phone went dead. She was going to stay right where she was and pray. Pray like she'd never prayed before.

'You're doing really, really well, Brianna,' the midwife declared encouragingly. 'Just a few more pushes and your first baby should be here.'

'Are…are the heart rates still OK?' Brianna gasped, trying to squint round at the monitor. 'No sign of any distress, abnormality?'

'Can you just concentrate on what you're supposed to be doing?' The midwife laughed. 'Honestly, you nurses and doctors make the worst possible mums-to-be. You know too much, that's the trouble. And, no, there's absolutely no sign whatsoever of either of your babies having difficulty,' she continued as Brianna made to interrupt. 'OK, another contraction's coming so work with it,' she added as Brianna let out a groan, and bore down hard.

'Is she OK?' Connor asked, his face chalk-white. 'My wife… Is she OK?'

'She's doing beautifully.'

'But it's been twelve hours,' Connor protested, wiping his forehead with one hand while holding onto Brianna's hand with the other. 'She's been in labour for twelve hours. Maybe you should be thinking of a Caesarean, or—'

'Shut…up…Connor,' Brianna said through her teeth. 'I…don't…want…a…oh…oh, my Lord…here comes another one.'

'Push, push,' the midwife ordered. 'The head's already out. We just need one more push, just one more, and… Oh, beautiful—just beautiful.' She beamed. 'You have a daughter, Brianna, a lovely daughter.'

'Is she all right?' Brianna asked, trying to lever herself upright, only to have to lie down again fast as another contraction rippled through her. 'Is she all right?'

'She's beautiful, Bree,' Connor said, his voice choked, his eyes shimmering. 'Just beautiful.'

But is she all right?' Brianna insisted.

'She's fine, just fine,' the midwife said reassuringly. 'You have a lovely, healthy, perfect baby. Now, keep on working with the contractions, keep working with them. I know you're very tired, but half the hospital staff seem to be outside in the corridor, desperately waiting for news, and we don't want to keep them waiting too much longer, do we?'

Brianna gripped Connor's hand again tightly, and heard him suck in his breath. He was going to be lucky to survive this without having any broken fingers, she thought, but the chuckle which would have broken from her was cut off as yet another contraction swept over her.

'Number two is on its way,' the midwife announced. 'Breathe with the pain, Brianna, go with it—don't fight it.'

'I'm…not…fighting…it,' Brianna protested, her face scarlet, her forehead beaded with sweat. 'I'm really not. I'm just…oh…oh, my…this is…'

'Hard,' Connor finished for her. 'I know it is, but you can do it, Bree. I can see the head crowning. You can do this. I know you can.'

And Brianna took a deep breath, and, with a harsh, guttural cry, pushed for all she was worth, and heard the midwife give an ecstatic whoop.

'She's here, Brianna. You have another little girl, and how you're ever going to tell your daughters apart… My heavens, they're like two peas in a pod, and the spitting image of their father.'

'Is she all right?' Brianna demanded. 'Is she…is she all right, too?'

'Absolutely,' the midwife announced.

For Brianna, all she wanted was to make sure her daughters were all right, to see for herself that they really and truly were all right, and when the midwife finally placed one of the babies in her arms she glanced quickly across at Connor and saw he was crying.

Crying and smiling at the same time, as he held their other daughter in his arms. A baby who was just as pink and healthy-looking as the one Brianna was holding. A baby who was breathing normally, and not erratically. A baby whose little face was screwed up in protest. Brianna let out a hiccupping laugh. A laugh that was pure relief and joy.

'Can I let the crowd outside in the corridor know the good news?' the midwife asked. 'The way they've been staked out all day, refusing to budge, you'd think these two babies were theirs. And, of course, they'll want to come in and see them, but…' She looked from Brianna to Connor, and smiled. 'Not yet, I think. The next few minutes are just for you. All four of you.'

And quickly the midwife bustled out the door, and Connor carefully placed the baby he was holding into Brianna's other arm, then sat down on the bed beside her.

'Oh, Bree, just look at them,' he said huskily. 'They are

just so…so…*beautiful*. And she's wrong—the midwife's wrong—they both look like you.'

'And Harry—they look like Harry, too, don't they?' Brianna said with an unsteady smile. 'I never thought this day would ever come, Connor. I never thought I would ever be able to think of Harry and smile. Every time I thought about him, I'd feel as though my heart was being ripped to pieces, but now… I just wish he could have been here, to see his little sisters, but I'm so grateful we had him even for that very short time.'

'I know,' he said softly. 'I feel the same way.' And then he laughed as an eruption of applause broke out in the corridor outside. 'Sounds like the midwife's just told everyone the good news.'

'We'll have to let them in soon, but do you realise we haven't even chosen names for our daughters?' Brianna declared. 'I didn't want to even think about names in case… you know…'

'Rhianna,' Connor said. 'I'd like to call one of them Rhianna, after your mother, if that's OK?'

'I'd like that, and I know she will.' Brianna nodded. 'And Aisling. Can we call our other daughter Aisling after your mother?''

'Are you sure?' Connor said unsteadily. 'It's a pretty old-fashioned sort of a name—'

'It's a beautiful name,' Brianna interrupted, planting a kiss on the top of each of her daughters' heads. 'Aisling and Rhianna. Our children.'

Connor delved into his pocket, and pulled out his wallet. For a second he stared down at it, then he carefully extracted a photograph and propped it up on the cabinet beside her.

'Aisling and Rhianna and Harry,' he said huskily. 'Our three beloved children.'

Tears welled in Brianna's eyes as she looked at the photograph.

'I didn't know you had that. You never said—never told me.'

'I took the photograph just after Harry was born, never thinking that…' He shook his head. 'And I couldn't throw it away, though even though looking at it always gave me pain, because it would have felt like I was throwing him away. I would have shown it to you, but…I thought…'

'I know.' She smiled tremulously. 'I know what you thought.'

From outside the labour ward they could hear the sound of raised voices, and Connor sighed.

'Sounds like they're getting restless out there,' he observed. 'Are you ready to let them in to see the new additions to the Monahan family?'

Brianna gazed down at her two daughters, then up at him.

'With you at my side, I'll always be ready for anything.'

And after Connor bent his head and kissed her, then slid off the bed to open the labour-ward door, Brianna glanced at the photograph on the bedside table and smiled.

'I love you, Harry,' she whispered. 'And I always will.'

Medical Romance™

ST PIRAN'S: PRINCE ON THE CHILDREN'S WARD
by Sarah Morgan

Children's doctor Tasha O'Hara's new job is looking after a sinfully gorgeous, injured Mediterranean prince. This isn't just *any* prince, but heartbreaker Prince Alessandro Cavalieri. Alessandro's definition of No Physical Activity *definitely* goes against doctor's orders…and it's becoming impossible for Tasha not to succumb to temptation!

HARRY ST CLAIR: ROGUE OR DOCTOR?
by Fiona McArthur

Harry St Clair does a good job persuading people that the devil-may-care rogue is the real him, but midwife Bonnie McKenzie isn't fooled! The real Harry St Clair is one of the best doctors in the southern hemisphere. The real Harry St Clair is buried under the weight of his devastating secrets—a weight he no longer has to carry alone…

On sale from 3rd June 2011
Don't miss out!

Available at WHSmith, Tesco, ASDA, Eason and all good bookshops
www.millsandboon.co.uk

0511/03b

are proud to present our...

Book of the Month

Come to Me
by Linda Winstead Jones

from Mills & Boon® Intrigue

Lizzie needs PI Sam's help in looking for her lost
half-sister. Sam's always had a crush on Lizzie.
But moving in on his former partner's daughter
would be *oh-so-wrong*...

Available 15th April

Something to say about our Book of the Month?
Tell us what you think!

Meet the three Keyes sisters—in Susan Mallery's unmissable family saga

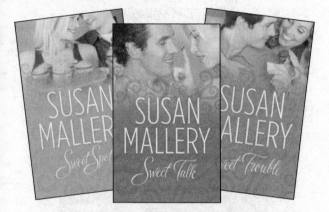

Sweet Talk
Available 18th March 2011

Sweet Spot
Available 15th April 2011

Sweet Trouble
Available 20th May 2011

For "readers who can't get enough of Nora Roberts' family series"—Booklist

MILLS
BOON

www.millsandboon.co.uk

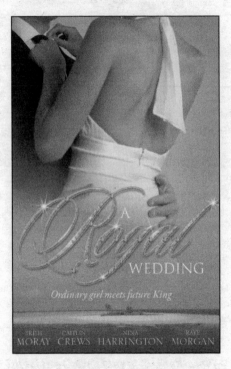

2 FREE BOOKS
AND A SURPRISE GIFT

We would like to take this opportunity to thank you for reading this Mills & Boon® book by offering you the chance to take TWO more specially selected books from the Medical™ series absolutely FREE! We're also making this offer to introduce you to the benefits of the Mills & Boon® Book Club™—

- **FREE home delivery**
- **FREE gifts and competitions**
- **FREE monthly Newsletter**
- **Exclusive Mills & Boon Book Club offers**
- **Books available before they're in the shops**

Accepting these FREE books and gift places you under no obligation to buy, you may cancel at any time, even after receiving your free books. Simply complete your details below and return the entire page to the address below. You don't even need a stamp!

YES Please send me 2 free Medical books and a surprise gift. I understand that unless you hear from me, I will receive 5 superb new stories every month including two 2-in-1 books priced at £5.30 each and a single book priced at £3.30, postage and packing free. I am under no obligation to purchase any books and may cancel my subscription at any time. The free books and gift will be mine to keep in any case.

Ms/Mrs/Miss/Mr _____ Initials _____

Surname _____

Address _____

_____

_____ Postcode _____

E-mail _____

Send this whole page to: Mills & Boon Book Club, Free Book Offer, FREEPOST NAT 10298, Richmond, TW9 1BR